THE GLOW

LEO X. ROBERTSON

The Glow
© 2022 Leo X. Robertson

www.aurelialeo.com

Robertson, Leo X.
The Glow / by Leo X. Roberston 1st ed.
ISBN-13: 978-1-946024-42-8 (ebook)
ISBN-13: 978-1-954541-17-7 (paperback)
Library of Congress Control Number: 2022944681

Editing by Lesley Sabga
Cover design by The Cover Collection (www.thecovercollection.com)
Book design by Knight Designs (authorzknight.com)

Printed in the United States of America
First Edition:
10 9 8 7 6 5 4 3 2 1

CHAPTER 1

I left Southend Central Station, instantly greeted by the visual equivalent of "What the hell were you thinking coming here, Lily?"

More than half the people in the crowd before me wore a t-shirt and white jeans, goose pimples from the harsh wind erupting across their arms.

Glowfolk.

On their t-shirts was a pink symbol like a stubby-fingered hand with a circle for a palm. It was the shape of the Glow's island, the mass of reconstituted plastic in the North Sea, downstream the Thames estuary, where their nefarious leaders resided. Here on land, Glowfolk walked twice as fast as anyone else, with open-mouthed grins and eyes that stared straight forward.

I looked up, determined not to meet anyone's gaze. Decaying boards covered up the building fronts before me, aimless sprays of graffiti coating the wood. Paper blew through the streets like fallen blossoms. I watched as they gathered in corners and gutters and got mashed into the pavement. Some pieces stopped at my feet. Miniature joker cards.

As I took all this in, a Glow member accosted me. Rail-thin, clothes hanging off him, blond hair stuck to his wide forehead.

"Welcome." He spoke in a calculatedly soothing voice and tugged on my sleeve.

I met his eyes. The irises were so dark that they blended with the pupils. Two big wet empty holes. No one home.

"No!" someone screamed.

Behind me, a frailer male Glow member had approached a woman who'd just gotten off the train. They wrestled over the bag. She eventually yanked it back from the man and walked briskly away.

Why don't I have the same intuitive resources?

I gripped my own suitcase tighter and held it close to my chest, a barrier between me and this weird world.

The guy in front of me grabbed my hand, prying the fingers from the suitcase handle and shaking it. His hand was freezing. "You're home now, I hope!"

"Do I know you?" I jerked my hand away and dug the nails into my palm to focus myself. I looked down at my chipped pink nail polish.

"Is this your only bag?" he asked.

"Please don't touch my—"

"Oh it's no trouble. I'll get it for you." Before I could say anything, he picked it up. "So where am I taking you?" He pointed a thumb over his shoulder. "We'll shoot on up to the compound. Why wouldn't we? Free accommodation, plenty of space for you. Don't need to bother with the hotels around here."

"But I'm already staying at the—" *Don't tell him.* "I've made my own arrangements. Thank you."

He placed a hand to one side of his mouth. "The hotels around here aren't that great!" He laughed, winked and winged out an elbow like I was supposed to latch onto him. "Come on, then. Let's go."

2

"Hey!" A large policewoman approached and grabbed him by the shoulder.

He shrugged her off and placed a hand where she'd touched him. "Ouch!"

Half a dozen other Glowfolk filtered out the crowd and surrounded the policewoman. They connected in a circle around her, arms pressed up against one another, and they guided her away while chanting "Shame! Shame! Shame!"

She shouted to me, "Don't go with him!" then got on her radio, calling for backup.

The police were clearly outnumbered here.

I picked up my suitcase and ran in the opposite direction from the shame circle, the unexpected exercise of it making my head pulse achingly.

The dead-eyed man called to me, but I turned a corner onto the main street.

"We lost her, thanks to you!" I heard the man say, in a darker voice than before.

———

Mum had taken me and my sister Joanna here on holiday when we were teens. At that age, we'd been more interested in heading to London. In the evening, when the day's gallivant to the aquarium or stroll down the pier had tired Mum out, and she wanted to retire to the B&B and read her book, Joanna and I would take the train to the city and head out to clubs in Shoreditch. We spent our summers sleeping in bus stations, changing in toilets on the train, and using lockers at the stations to store our overnight kits.

This Southend-on-Sea wasn't the same place that we'd sobered up in at six a.m., cooling off our hangovers on the beach with free ice cream obtained by flirting with that summer's awkward teen vendor.

The street I turned onto was packed. Vagrants walked by

in bulky stained jackets that reeked of alcohol and old cigarette smoke, talking to themselves. On their backs were sleeping bags tied with twine and stained hiking rucksacks. They were old beyond their years in the face: craggy skin, missing teeth. Some carted around trolleys full of plastic, likely heading to a recycling center. That was a common "living" here. The Glow's own efforts in this arena were why no one bothered them for the longest time.

Once again, most shop fronts were boarded up. Those that remained—cafés, hairdressers, clothes shops—all had white signs with pink letters on them.

Posters coated the windows of closed-down bars and chip shops. They advertised "Workshops with the Advanced Efficacy Group" and "Self-Actualization Solutions." The Glow had many more of these "businesses", each a component of one whole that denied its connection with the other parts, allowing their organization to shapeshift like an amoeba, retracting some parts and growing others to evade toxic blame.

A torn image of Gabriel Brooks advertised acting classes with Excalibur School. I liked him, how he'd kept doing indie films even as his career picked up. He'd remained an Authentic, hadn't sold his likeness to any of the major studios, who were likely clamoring to digitally insert him into just about anything. He was one of the remaining few whose appearance in a film was a sign of its quality.

And he'd gone missing months ago.

I shuddered, but not for the cold. My whole body urged me to get out of here, but I had nowhere better to be.

I found my hotel, waited for a gap in the stream of people walking past, and headed inside.

The check-in desk was an empty steel booth with a bunch of grubby touchscreens around the wall. I went to one and tapped in all my details. A smiling cartoon female welcomed me but warned me that they had methods of detecting "overnight guests."

My room was nondescript and beige: bed, mirror, cupboard, desk, iron, kettle with cups and drink sachets. I searched the cupboards for a minibar, disappointed to find nothing more exciting than a fridge with two small water bottles inside.

I flopped down on the bed. The trip here, and my instant encounter with the Glow upon arrival, had exhausted me. I soon fell asleep in my clothes.

———

The Glow got our attention when a meteorite landed on their island.

There's footage of it, a rainbow streak in the night sky, a flash of white light like burning magnesium landing on that jagged, painful-looking mass of plastic.

As far as anyone could tell, the island didn't melt, nor did the meteorite drop through its base. Why not? Wasn't the island plastic after all?

Rookie journalists flew their drones out to the island—but marksmen, standing atop the island's plastic towers, slung the drones into the sea with fishing rods.

Truthers set up blogs of blurry GIFs that noted angles of approach, terminal velocities, tenuous connections between apparent shapes and the usual suspect shadow organizations.

In my less proud evenings—subdued by the mash of kratom leaves lodged in my cheek—I'd spend hours browsing these sites, gleaning and collating anything remotely resembling evidence. Whenever I did understand what the bloggers were talking about, I could tell it was wrong.

But it resonated with me all the same. I was on their weirdo wavelength. The intent of their sites amused me more than the content. I asked the same questions that fueled their misguided curiosities. The idea that everything I saw was the extent of reality was far more terrible than any truther's proposal, no matter how outlandish. How reassuring it would be to discover at least that yes, there are secrets, even if I'd never know what they were.

I remained skeptical, but conspiracy theorists kept convincing themselves that some alien intelligence had selected the Glow to be the vanguard of its cosmic secrets.

The island appeared on the news each night. A floating neon Kraken, lit up by a "bioluminescent phytoplankton lighting system." Gentle pinks and purples that pulsed like an engorged, extra-terrestrial heart.

Something had landed there and changed everything. But the Glow would never let us know what it was.

I so badly wished this was nothing more than curious office banter for me, that I could pontificate on theories with pure objectivity. But Joanna was gone, and I had reason to suspect she was on the island, dining on Venusian grapes, banging on an octopus-skin tambourine and praying to Cthulhu.

Tomorrow, I'd go there and find out if she was.

CHAPTER 2

My watch rang, waking me up. If anything, I felt groggier than before.

It was five fourteen in the afternoon. I knew because it was Henry calling. He'd come home, searched the house and found that I wasn't there.

I pressed on the watch face and propped it up on the nightstand. "Hey babe, what's up?"

His black quiff was lopsided, dark bags gathering beneath his eyes. He adjusted the dial in his jaw for volume, said nothing for a full minute, and then, "Shit."

"You know me so well."

"Get back here now!"

I examined my nails. "I'm going to the island tomorrow."

Why did I tell him that? I hated thinking that far ahead. Coming here was tough—but the idea of getting in a boat, I assumed, and careening into the open water, was enough to make me hyperventilate.

I shook my head to rid myself of the idea.

He stuttered through his words, likely trying to think of ways to discourage me—then sighed, knowing he couldn't. "You don't know how to get there."

"But you do."

He clicked his tongue. "Aubrey Millar, Saira Kinney, Fred McGrath. Off the top of my head. Cases I worked on. Gone. And that's just in Ipswich. How many more would you guess the island has claimed in the whole country? And beyond?" He ran his fingers through his hair. "Is this because of what I said last night?"

"You know how to get there."

He went silent.

Wow. I was just guessing.

Here he went again, protecting me how he saw fit, rather than how I needed. Or so I knew he would claim. Which I thought was just an excuse for the probable complex he'd inherited from his dad, a condescending desire to protect us gentle womenfolk from the big scary world.

One can only imagine what that did to my desire to reach the island.

"Talk to me, Lily," he said finally.

"This is worse than cheating."

"You think I'd help you out with this?" Blue light spread across his face. A computer screen. He looked at it, reading something. "You've got a forty-three percent chance of coming back if you stay there one day. Ten percent after two days. Zero after three. Best case scenario, they'll recruit you, even with everything you know. We don't know enough to say what the worst case is." He looked back at me then quickly away again, as if he couldn't face my gaze. "I can't talk to you when you're like this. But you've made your point. You can come back now. I'll help."

"*Now?*"

"Well I never thought you had the strength to just up and leave. This is a real breakthrough for you. I like it. I knew you had potential, but—"

"You were holding me back?"

He forced a laugh, which went on for too long. "God, how ungrateful you are."

It was a relief hearing him talk to me like this. I'd always known he wanted to. Seeing the state of Southend-on-Sea had me thinking my domestic life wasn't that bad. As Henry now proved, it wasn't much better.

"Hey, I'm curious," he said.

"Go on."

"I get that Joanna's your sister. But she's not the only one on that island. And how many times on the news have you seen families accept, with dignity, that rescue attempts are too risky?"

"Just because they don't go out there, doesn't mean they've accepted it. And anyway, I owe it to her."

"Why?"

I considered this. Maybe it was because I could see clearly, in retrospect, Joanna's path in life towards the Glow and the island.

For one, there was that ritual she'd proposed we perform together for her eighteenth birthday. She'd read about it online. Three days of meditating, fasting, walking backwards blindfolded and other strange activities. It said she was to invite the person to whom she felt closest. But I'd tried to get her to laugh it off. It sounded dangerous.

She said nothing more to me and left by herself, only to return later the same day.

After that incident, I thought she was done. But I'd go to her bedroom to talk to her and she'd be on her bed wearing tie-dye harem pants, listening to a woman chanting over strange atonal music and reading some oddly sized book, a psychedelic mandala or Magic Eye image on its shiny cover. The author, in his black and white photo, was always an older man with skin lined like bark, with wiry hair and thick seventies glasses.

She'd see me take all this in and say nothing. Our conversation would become stilted. I'd squandered my chance to talk openly with her about these interests.

So why did I owe it to Joanna to seek her out? Because she'd been silently suffering and I'd given her reasons not to look for me as an outlet and now it was almost, almost too late to do anything.

I didn't feel like telling this to Henry.

He shouted to regain my attention: "Lily!"

Were those tears?

"You don't think about anyone but yourself, do you?" he said. "Putting yourself in danger. Giving up everything! It's like you don't even care that—"

"You're starting to get it." What my frustration with Joanna was like, I meant.

He looked at me with blank eyes. "Call it a last favor—but if I don't hear from you in the next forty-eight hours, I'm coming out there myself."

I hung up.

We could easily have avoided speaking to each other like that, if only either of us had addressed the resentment earlier. Instead I just sat every evening watching the Crevasse of the Unsaid expand between us. I treated our relationship like a house plant I'd stopped caring for, thinking it was easier to watch it die than bother resuscitating it.

He might not tell me how to get to the island, but at least he wasn't going to send anyone to stop me. Did he know me well enough to understand that I'd see it as a loving gesture?

I took a shower, but made it quick and I slathered myself with lotion afterwards. The water in this area was highly caustic.

I then got dressed and headed to the bar downstairs.

CHAPTER 3

Behind the bar was a buff guy in a black t-shirt. A real human for once, old school. He had a nice face, strong cheekbones, but the tattoos on his arms were ropy. Once they must have been black, now they were dark green, their shapes bled and muddy.

A punky couple sat on the stools at the other end of the bar. The woman had steel gauges in her ears, pink hair and wore a torn black denim jacket. The man had a beard and crew cut hair, gold rings on his hands and a tattoo on his neck of a bloody knuckle duster.

Together, the couple and bartender watched the news on a small screen propped up on a shelf.

Dennis Howell—the bleached and tightened suit closest to what passed for the Glow's spokesman—spoke to a morning show host, who was offscreen. He was addressing allegations that drug-fueled violence in the Southend area was the Glow's fault. "Our task forces dredge plastic out the ocean and use innovative in-house technologies to extract it from fish that would otherwise die. We remove cancer-causing organochlorines and phthalates from the waters. All of this at a time when it's clear that the government has failed to take care of these issues itself. Not to mention the purpose we've given numerous members." He looked right into the camera, as if talking directly to me. "The last thing we need for the kind of complicated and creative work we do is a set of drug abusers or subservient drones. We extol individual responsibility."

The bartender stood between me and the screen. "What can I get for you, miss?"

"Sorry, I didn't mean to—I wasn't—"

"It's okay."

With how quickly he'd accepted my apology, he'd obviously expected it. But what was I sorry for? And how had he, this random bartender, managed to elicit this desired response from me? If I couldn't spot that—

It didn't bear thinking about. "Double gin and tonic, please," I said to him.

He tilted his head with concern. "You had dinner yet?" Perhaps another sales tactic, but incidentally a welcome suggestion.

"What's good?"

"The burger's safe. A quality synthetic."

"One of those then."

I beeped my wrist on the credit reader. I had about three days' worth of cash before I hit the limit. The Glow had nothing but debt to steal from me.

After ringing up the order, he brought me a glass with ice and cucumber in it. He held a bottle of Hendrick's Gin. "Say when." He winked and started to pour.

I looked at him in the eyes as the gin sloshed upwards: a quarter-glass, a half.

His face changed. He stopped pouring and gave me the tonic bottle. "Don't think it'll fit now. You can top up as you go, I guess."

"Yeah whatever."

"So what brings you to the last non-Glow hotel in town?"

"Southend's aquarium."

His laugh was gravelly. He shook his head then went through to the kitchen.

I sipped my drink. It was like perfume, too strong. I probably couldn't drink it all if I was serious about finding out how to get to the island tomorrow.

When the bartender returned, the couple both ordered beers.

"She was homeless at first," the woman said. "Everyone knows that. Whether she was on drugs is debatable."

It made sense that everyone here would be talking about the island or its supposed leader, Patricia, all the time. The topic cropped up back in Ipswich on occasion, but usually in some hackneyed joke told by a co-worker or late-night talk show host on TV.

I asked if they were talking about Patricia.

"Yeah!" the woman said. "We're journalists with The Switch."

"Oh yeah. I watched your report on illegal drone mods. Heath and Corinne, right?"

"But don't tell anyone!" Corinne said. "And your name?"

"Lily. Are you both covering the Glow, then?"

Heath nodded. Corinne slapped his arm, but he looked at her reassuringly. Why else, after all, would they be here?

"You discovered anything so far?" I asked.

Heath smiled at me. "I guess we can give a fan a preview. Maybe you saw all those joker cards all over the street."

The mashed muddy blossoms strewn across the roadsides, one of the first things I'd noticed upon arrival.

"They're laced with drugs," he continued. "That's why they're 'joker cards.' Play them and opt out of life. We sent some to a lab and they confirmed traces of octadrone. The Glow make it in their compound. It's a highly addictive stimulant that gets absorbed on skin contact. So they use them in their rituals. They get members hooked to prevent them from leaving, because the Glow control the production and supply." He played with the gold ring on his middle finger. "Apart from that, not much else. We interviewed a whole bunch of members, but it's like talking to the same person a dozen times."

"I've got to say, I'm glad I met you both. Back in Ipswich, the Glow's just a bad joke."

I lost my job for that very reason. A woman at work had been crying in the bathroom. Her family's neighborhood in Mumbai had flooded and she couldn't get in touch with anyone to check if they were okay. I tried to comfort her by telling her about my sister. She laughed and said, "Thanks, I needed cheering up"—so I slapped her in the face.

After that, I'd run out of reasons not to come here.

"This place is insane," I continued, "But better to be here and look at it than to deny it."

Did I agree with that, or did I just want to be heard saying it?

Corinne nodded in approval. "You're here for someone."

"My sister. She's in the Glow."

"Oh really?"

I folded my arms and rested them on the bar. "Joanna had this blog where she'd post inspirational quotes, self-care advice, the auditions she'd been on in London, some promo stuff for the cocktail place she worked at. The posts get progressively darker. She writes every day about every little failing—no callbacks, skin breakouts, envy—each post filled with attempts at self-deprecation that miss the mark. Total Glow bait when I think about it. She starts writing about how to handle anxiety and depression, and then just full-on depression, depression, depression. I reach out to her when I can, post books to her, tell her I'll come down to see her some weekend. She responds less and less." I peeled the leather of my jacket where it had stuck to a spill. "I notice this one blogger replying to all of my sister's posts. Lengthy, repetitive ramblings about how important my sister's work is to her.

She hints at some method she knows of that eradicates all doubt."

"Ding ding," Corinne said.

I nodded. "This other blogger writes, 'Sent you a private message.' That's the last of her and Joanna's public correspondence. And Joanna stops posting after that."

"A familiar story," Corinne said. "I take it you have more evidence that connects your sister to the Glow though?"

"Not really. My mum told me too late that she'd called the Glow's hotline."

Heath and Corinne winced.

"The first time Glowfolk showed up at Mum's house, she called the police to report harassment and they took a statement. The next ten times they said they were 'aware of the issue, working on it.' The last time she called, an officer sighed and said, 'Join the club.'" I took a straw and poked at the ice in my drink, watching the bubbles that resulted. "My sister's on the island."

I looked away. I wouldn't be here unless I'd fully exhausted the option of lying to myself, but I couldn't yet face their reactions. It would make it too real all at once.

"Hey," Corinne said, "we've talked to so many people in your position who've lost family members to the Glow. It's very common for them to think they know someone on the island. But there are far more Glowfolk than just the ones out there. The chances of—"

"I know it."

Corinne thought she was helping me, but she was attacking something for which I'd worked hard: my acceptance that Joanna was on the island. One best-case scenario I'd considered was that I went out there and didn't find Joanna, then I could be pleasantly surprised, because perhaps she wasn't as far gone as I'd imagined. But would it really be better if I couldn't find her at all?

"'Call it intuition,' huh?" Corinne said. "I've heard that too."

I looked at them with desperation. "You're going out there, aren't you?"

"Lily," Heath said, "together we've investigated police brutality, cybercrime, biological warfare. Murders in space. And been everywhere all that entails." He leaned in. "There's no way we're going to that island."

The bartender returned with my burger. He loudly cleared his throat as he placed it down beside me. On the plate was a napkin on which he'd written, in black pen, *Wait until they leave.*

Corinne stared at him, then broke her thought and turned to me, smiling. "Thanks for sharing with us, Lily. Best of luck finding your sister."

"Sure," I said after a straw full of cold straight gin. "Hope your report turns out great."

They finished their drinks and got up. I turned to watch them walk away, and downed the rest of my glass.

I wished I was part of some edgy, like-minded couple. Myself and some tatted up journalist deigning to come here for our entertainment, under the guise of worthwhile reporting.

I heard liquid sloshing into a glass. The bartender gave me a refill and poured his own measure of gin.

"I thought they'd never leave." He lifted his glass and clinked it against mine, winking.

"What are we toasting?"

"Your arrival on the island."

"Hah."

He went to get another napkin and took a pen from his pocket. "This is us." He sketched a square for the hotel. "Behind us are the piers." He sketched them. "At six a.m. tomorrow, go to the gate here and give the waiting Glowperson this."

He took a shot glass from behind the bar. In it were several new joker cards.

"How did you…?" I reached for one.

"Ah ah ah! Didn't you hear what that pair said?"

I was so naïve, still. Why had I assumed these wouldn't have the drug on them?

I wrapped the sleeve of my jacket over my hand, picked one up and put it in my pocket.

"Tomorrow morning, walk up to Pier 8 and meet Melodie by her plastic powerboat. You can't miss it."

I was up against addictive stimulants and brainwashing techniques that had worked on, what, tens of thousands of members worldwide? And the Glow had a year-long head start on me, I estimated, based on the last I heard from Joanna. So my mission didn't have much hope from the start. The less I thought of that, the better. All the same, each day away from Joanna counted. Every day was another chance to pull her back out. Every day, she sank in deeper. This whole town was designed either to repel or eliminate me.

What reason had I to believe this stranger wasn't part of that same twisted ecosystem?

What other leads did I have?

"How do you know all this?" I asked him, still without reason to believe any answer he gave.

He tapped the side of his nose.

"Why are you telling only me?"

"You want your sister back, don't you?"

If you could feel the ache inside me, you wouldn't even ask.

I'd been suppressing any joy at the prospect of actually succeeding at getting Joanna back, given how unlikely it was. But thanks to the bartender's prompt, it briefly broke through. Drunken tears formed too easily in my eyes. I climbed onto the stool and hugged him around his neck. "Thank you."

He let me hug him. "Room 395, was it?" His breath was hot against my neck.

I released him and looked in his eyes.

"I can pay now," I said. "I think I have enough credit for another anyway." Though I'd already figured he wasn't talking about the bar tab.

I tried to tap my wrist to the reader but he took my hand away and enveloped it in his. "This one's on me."

I swallowed, hard. "Very kind of you. I'll finish it in my room."

He tutted. "Can't allow that."

I yanked my hand from his. "Then I'll leave it here."

I walked away, feeling his eyes burning on my back.

———

Back in my room, I locked the door. When I saw that the chain was broken, I took off my trainers and wedged them in the gap at the bottom.

I filled the kettle with bottled water from the minibar and turned it on, placing a coffee sachet in a cup. As I waited, I undressed down to t-shirt and pants, then poured the water on the coffee, taking the mug to the bed, where I sat cross-legged.

I turned off the bedside light and sat there in the darkness.

Sure enough, I later saw feet beneath the door. The handle rattled and I heard someone muttering under their breath.

CHAPTER 4

The morning air chilled me as I walked along the pier, trailing my suitcase behind me. I stopped to chew on a mouthful of kratom to give me confidence for the journey, looking up at the old rollercoaster and big wheel of my early holidays. It was rusted now and cast long shadows through the gathering mist.

Crouched shapes, like mournful statues, revealed more homeless people in their big jackets as I approached them. I'd thought myself one of the few awake at this hour. They ground their teeth and talked to themselves. Maybe they were addicted to that drug, like Heath explained last night.

I reached the gate at Pier 8 almost out-of-body. To come here after hearing Henry's prognosis of survival, those diminishing percentages per day spent on the island, I'd had to shut off my intuition and walk towards danger. Which surely made me great cult fodder.

A young woman stood there in a white plastic smock with the stubby-fingered hand on it. She held a clipboard, suggesting she controlled everything along the pier.

"Hi!" Her expression mimicked that of an old friend, but her dead eyes revealed the falseness of the conceit. "What can

I showed her the joker card.

"Great!"

What would've happened if I didn't have this? She was rake-thin, but if there was any truth to the Glow's teachings, she'd tapped into hidden power reserves.

She looked at her notes and wrote something down. "You're the fourth today."

"Already? Wow. You expecting more?"

"Fingers crossed!" She giggled. "Please go right ahead to Slip 903 on the left, where Melodie will be more than happy to receive you."

I nodded and continued.

I couldn't see that far in front of me at all. Where was Melodie supposed to be? Was there a "Melodie", or was "being received by Melodie" Glow lingo for making someone disappear?

I walked past innocuous yachts, houseboats, catamarans, wondering which one I was supposed to wait beside—and then I saw her, sitting in a ragged approximation of a powerboat.

She had long center-parted blonde hair and wore a plastic poncho. I leaned closer to examine her boat, seeing melted milk bottles, jags of blue and pink pallets, food packaging and plastic bags. It was made from scavenged and reconstituted bits of plastic.

Melodie smiled at me. "So happy you could join us." She sounded like she'd just woken up. Low energy, a waif of a girl.

Behind her was a stocky kid wearing a gold-spiked baseball cap, thick black glasses and a black denim jacket with embroidered gold insignia on the back, muffin-topping out his skinny jeans. Beside him were two teenage girls, one taller than the other, both with long black hair and angular gold jewelry on their wrists. They wore short white puffer jackets with gloves sewn on the inner lining. Their belly rings were showing. They'd brought only small backpacks, which made me feel silly as I negotiated getting my suitcase into the boat.

"Can you come here for a second?" Melodie said to me.

I stumbled into the boat, balancing myself by gripping onto the slip's metal cleat.

I approached Melodie and she felt my face.

The teenagers laughed.

"I'm checking for e-implants," Melodie said. "We don't allow them on the island."

Strange. They didn't have to be on the face anymore, though I wasn't about to tell her that. Luckily the Glow remained out of touch.

"They creep me out," I said.

She laughed mildly, which relieved me a little.

"My boyfriend has a gabber jaw," I continued. "One of those facial phone things. Conducts sound through his skull."

"Oh yeah?" she said.

"Freaks me out. No one needs to get in touch with me *that* urgently."

No laughter, no sound at all.

Shouldn't have said that, I thought.

I heard murmuring behind me.

When Melodie was done with my face, I turned to see Heath and Corinne, holding hands.

"Who told you?" I said.

They lowered their heads.

"The bartender," Heath said. "Before you arrived. He said not to tell anyone. People ask him about it all the time and he's sad to see so many—"

"He told me after you left." I folded my arms. "He wanted to come up to my room."

Corinne came forward and held my hands. "I'm so sorry. We were naïve."

So am I, I thought, but I said, "Bodes well for your survival."

Had I insulted Melodie? She didn't react.

"God," Corinne said, "and after everything you told me about your sister."

I didn't think that had bothered me until she brought it up. Everyone I'd met before them had collectively lowered my expectations. But no, I didn't just tell anyone about the growing distance between me and my sister, not anymore. I'd told Corinne and her husband because I respected them. It seemed, unfortunately, that I had expected more from them.

I'd try not to do that again.

Would I just keep getting further jaded or was it at all possible that Joanna and I would reunite at all, let alone soon? I dreaded finding out, and yet I had to.

"From here on out, we tell each other everything," Heath said.

I slouched. "Good idea."

"That's all I can take," Melodie said, as if mad that we expected more arrivals.

"Guess we're ready to go, then," Heath said.

He and Corinne climbed into the boat, which tilted precariously as it adjusted to the new weight. Once everyone was in, their faces felt for chips, Melodie sat by the motor. "Hold tight!"

She untethered the boat and we sped across the water.

———

"Did you see Gabe in *Edge of the Storm*?"

"You know him as 'Gabe', do you?"

"I will by the end of today!"

The three teenagers talked amongst one another. Corinne and Heath looked at me in disbelief, but I focused on the boat's floor, too nervous to look away.

The boy looked at Heath and said, "Fine then, if not for Gabriel Brooks, why are *you* going?"

"We want to meet Patricia, for one," Corinne said. "We don't think she exists."

"No matter why you're coming today," Melodie said, her expression unchanging, "I hope we get the chance to win you all over. We don't like eating up our biodiesel on these trips." She laughed nervously.

Was biodiesel as pungent when burnt as what I could now smell? I figured it wouldn't be since it came from vegetable oil—typically, always?—but maybe that was ignorant of me.

"Of course," Corinne said. "We appreciate it. We meant no disrespect."

Melodie didn't reply. She hardly blinked and tears fell down her face. The cold sea wind, or something else? I had no idea. If something about that interaction had just gone badly wrong for Melodie, I didn't know what it was. It made me wonder what I might say, or not say, on the island, and what the consequences would be. Again, no idea.

Melodie felt me watching her and nodded ahead to redirect my attention.

There it was. Between the looming wind farms, those forests of metal poles and turbines in the sea. Beyond hulking cargo ships, which breezed aimlessly by, carting around their dull-colored shipping containers. A pale plastic Kremlin. Four large towers with onion bulb heads and other spheres along their length at regular intervals like nodules on a plant root. Together, the towers looked like the swollen-jointed fingers of an enormous, gout-wracked hand.

A glow of pastel light stole up the towers like ivy. Clusters of tendrils made a fluorescent octopus shape in the center of a plaza, around which the towers crowded. It was the plastic mold of a place's memory. A castle's ghost.

As I observed the island for the first time, I almost forgot what planet I was on. And the Glow made that much more sense to me. What better place for a "new lifestyle" than somewhere that didn't look like anywhere else on Earth, completely isolated from the rest of the world? A place that looked deserving of its own rules and strange new commitments. New ways to honor its weird beauty.

The sight hit my heart in a way that felt entirely unfamiliar, but not unpleasant.

As we approached, the island's shapes gained definition. The delicate crenellations of the towers, their ragged cellophane windows. The white plastic of the buildings and the mess of pink plant parts intertwined like teeth embedded in rotting gums.

The front of more buildings appeared through the mist at sea level: houses, barns, studies. Where the cement of their surfaces had eroded, light shone through plastic bottles wired together.

Out here, plastic was a prized currency.

———

We reached the island's harbor, its four flea-bitten plastic piers. A translucent tentacle rose from the pier beside us, glowing with pink light. It slunk into the boat and curled into its side, pulling it close to the pier, light running up and down it in vascular pulses.

Marching feet squelched on wet ground.

Melodie tugged on a cord attached to the boat's motor and it sputtered to a stop. It was a key, ensuring only she could let us go.

We got out and approached the plaza, from which five petals—alleyways, living quarters and other buildings— branched off.

Heath, Corinne and I stole a surreptitious glance between us. As soon as our eyes met, we knew we had to look away again. This did not seem like a place tolerant of private communication, and it surely wasn't wise to demonstrate allegiances, friendships or anything that gave the Glow ammunition.

Glow members in plastic ponchos, perhaps fifty or so, filtered out of the lanes between the wonky buildings. The island bobbed gently, but they walked with experienced sea legs.

My stomach muscles tightened at the sight of them, as if holding in the dread. As if preparing to get punched.

But the Glow appeared nothing but friendly as they raised their arms up and chanted, "Welcome, welcome, welcome."

CHAPTER 5

The first wave of Glowfolk embraced us, their guests, with measured pressure.

The teenagers stood stiffly as poncho plastic rustled off their jackets. The heady smell of it, in the island's surprisingly humid environment, gave me something short of a migraine.

Glowfolk surrounded us, gently chanting something, swaying back and forth like anemone fronds, waving sparklers. As placid as they appeared, they were obviously malnourished. Smiles revealed teeth of mismatched color: those that had always been were darker than those replaced.

As objective as I was sure Heath and Corinne wanted to be, their faces took on parental looks of pity as they embraced Glow members. Like they wanted to scoop up all these sorry people and take them home.

The sparklers died, and the Glow swarmed us, settling us together in a sticky web of a hug, plastic crinkling in my ears.

"So glad to meet you," a woman with a messy bob said to me.

"I love your jacket, wow," said a tall man behind me, stroking my sleeve.

The teenagers smiled, trying not to giggle.

Heath smiled back at the members, while Corinne looked about to vomit.

I felt male hands inside my jacket, exploring the pockets therein, knuckles brushing past my breasts. I cringed and pulled my arms closer to my sides.

Excessive signs of protest on my part would surely not be received well. I'd already figured that—but what would I let the Glow do to me? If I'd taken that in, I probably wouldn't have come. I guessed I was thankful that I hadn't, then. Though that really depended on my progress on finding my sister.

A disappointment hit me in the gut that Joanna wasn't on the front line, as if by learning the identities of island Glow members, the chances of Joanna being out here diminished. The more new faces I took in, the more this feeling gripped me.

"Hey!" I said, pulling away, clutching my suitcase. I pushed out of the crowd and regained my breath. The zip on my bag was down. I pulled it back up.

Members stepped back, their feet padding on the mulchy floor. Between sharp ridges of microwaveable packaging, cassette tapes, fragments of old TVs and photo frames, were mounds of purple moss. Small clusters of some glowing, alien vegetation filled opportunistic holes like unattended warts left to thrive. Dead hermit crabs sloshed in the floor's crevices, in the water that pooled over the ragged edges. Beads of sunlight, in splashed seawater, shone upon the mottled plastic fabric. And yet the island smelled like a steam room, of a gentle clean fragrance entrained in thick water vapor.

The circle of Glowfolk receded and I had a chance to look around.

Chubby succulents lined the undulating floor and—not trees, but tree-shaped clumps of foreign vegetation, pulsing with light, encircled the plaza.

27

Mold-spotted shower curtains secured the doorways. Members sat cross-legged just outside them, plastic tubs in their laps, scrubbing clothes on hand-made plastic washboards in dark, soapy water.

Monolithic creepers ran up the plastic towers. The plants wound and wormed their way around them, spiraling towards weird amalgams of treehouses and small woven huts. Their chewed and reconstituted structures looked like the hives of alien wasps.

The members looked us up and down, taking us in. Beneath their colorful translucent ponchos, they wore regular comfy clothing: t-shirts, jumpers, joggers, harem pants and even pajama bottoms.

The teenagers had pushed through the crowd and collectively embraced a tall blond man who wore a fancier-looking tunic than the rest, made from iridescent plastic. It had to be Gabriel Brooks, I told myself, but it took an inordinate time to recognize him. He looked like he'd cut his own hair, and had something like liver spots on his face. I doubted they'd used that much Photoshop on his posters—in which case, how could anything that had aged him that much, that quickly, be good?

As I pondered this, someone hugged me from the side. I recognized the coconut scent, and inhaling it delivered a flood of favorite memories, of unfettered silliness, distilled life-affirmation.

A cheap flat warming party for her in London, with nuts and crisps in paper bowls because she hadn't bought any crockery yet, drinking champagne from plastic flutes and dancing to music on cheap phone speakers, getting messy and shouting "This is what it's all about!" Until we'd riled her neighbors.

Hanging out with the wrong crowd down the nature trail by the school, passing a can of deodorant between us and huffing solvents from it through a hand towel like a bunch of idiots.

Holding hands and running away from the wedding reception for her dad and our Mum.

That we were stepsisters didn't remove us from one another. We lasted longer than our fathers did with Mum. We were the ones those unions were supposed to bring together.

She released me. I turned to her. She was so pale I could barely see her freckles, her skin the same color as the long plastic tunic she wore. Her hair was its natural chestnut for the first time since she was thirteen. She resembled the skinny sixteen-year-old I'd force-fed apple slices and chocolate squares, with her jutting hips, angular elbows, emaciated face.

I hugged her again, swaying her from side to side.

"Welcome." She didn't sound like herself. "My name is Joy."

I'd guessed it would be unwise to reveal family connections to members on the island. Like that, we were instantly complicit. Unless she didn't remember me at all.

"Joy," I said. "Joy it is, then."

From across the plaza, where a tall pair of men welcomed the other visitors—the teens and journalists—to the island, Heath and Corinne looked at me. Despite myself, I met their gaze. Though we hadn't known each other long, I could tell they knew exactly what the shock and excitement in my eyes meant.

Shit.

I didn't want to give anything away. Even if they'd claimed they were on my side, I'd just met them and had no reason to trust anyone at all. I had to suppress all natural instincts, keep everything bottled up for the duration of my stay.

"You two seem to be getting along!" A woman walked up behind Joanna. She had a wind-weathered face, long ash-colored dreadlocks flecked with sea mist, and large wooden gauges in her ears.

"Lily, was it?" Joanna said to me.

She hadn't forgotten. Well, that quashed a worry I'd just developed, placing me just a step beneath square one.

"Meet my wife."

I let Joanna go and turned to this woman, shaking her hand.

"Ella," she said. She looked between us. "Joy gets a hug and I get a handshake?"

"It's so nice to meet you." I held her by the shoulders, looking between her and my sister. "I mean it."

"You've been lost a long time, huh?" Ella said. "It's okay. You're home now. Let go."

Of course I couldn't. I had to hold myself back and dry my eyes. They couldn't learn what got to my emotions, or anything further about me. As pleasant as they might have seemed, as normal as they wanted to pretend this place was, they were insidious.

As for Joanna, it was promising that she kept our connection secret. Over the time I spent here, I'd try to enhance our alliance, ideally reaching a tipping point where she would re-devote herself to family over the Glow. And then we could leave.

For now, I had to leave the name Joanna behind. For our safety.

CHAPTER 6

I left my suitcase by a low, wishbone-shaped table in the plaza. Around it were air-filled pillows made from melted foil packets. Up the back was a podium with a plastic throne in its center. Bright fronds rose from it and curled around its legs.

The table surrounded the meteorite. It was a bowling ball of mottled metal locked behind a plastic polygonal cage, sitting on a plinth of glowing plant flesh. It looked like the head of a viral particle. Pink glowing tendrils spread out from its central hub, metastasizing across the plaza and up its buildings. Their rainbow glow of bioluminescence lulled me like a lava lamp.

Behind a translucent plastic wall, marred with scratches and seams, a body lay on a plinth. What I assumed were clumps of the same glowing plant, on the wall behind her, lit her silhouette so we could see it here in the plaza. It was like looking at a frozen cavewoman through a dirty, warped glacier.

I peered closely. Patricia was breathing.

Or was it a plastic contraption made to look like a sleeping woman? The strategy of deferring authority to an invented leader had obvious perks.

Joanna playfully punched me on the arm.

"Ouch!"

"Have some respect! Don't stare."

"Noted." In a reflex I grinned at her like a misbehaving kid, but she wouldn't reciprocate.

A woman emerged from the shower curtain doorway of Patricia's room. She had short hair and wore a red turtleneck. Instead of a poncho, she had a toga, bedizened with chains of plastic jewelry.

"Let's get one thing clear," she said, pacing before the throne. "We're not a cult."

I wanted to laugh. *Why say that unless…?*

Heath made an involuntary sound then covered his mouth with a fist and pretended it was a cough.

With just four words she was in my head. Had she said them because they were a cult, or because they weren't? Their methods, if suspect, surely thrived in a mental landscape of confusion. She had an irritated frown and stood in an exaggerated pose as if defending from an unexpected attack

"Most of you will leave again," she continued, "having already made up your minds about us. To such people I have nothing to say other than, 'You're welcome to go.' We want the dreamers, the crusaders, the adventurers. And yes, the weirdos, fruitcakes and freaks. If you haven't fit in before, you might be made for our way of life. Like you, it has never existed before. You can only find it here and now."

The codependent in me had fired up, desperate to please this stranger by fulfilling her arbitrary criteria.

I wasn't ready for this.

She smiled now, her expression changed as if she'd flipped some internal switch. "I'm Summer, by the way."

An unnatural, machine-gun laugh erupted from the Glowfolk. It had me ducking to protect myself, rather than wanting to join in.

Summer sent Glowfolk rippling away from her as she

walked to the stone's cage, unlocking it with a key from one of her lock necklaces.

Corinne blinked rapidly at this. Either she couldn't believe her eyes or she'd managed to sneak an ocular e-implant past Glow security and now took photos.

Joanna poked me. "We rarely get to see the meteorite!"

Oh please! As if we're so special.

However many times visitors came out here—daily, weekly maybe—why wouldn't they do this each visit?

But I shot Joanna an encouraging grin out of habit. Over the years she'd learned that it was false. It was the same humoring look I'd given her kindergarten puppet performances, then later her one-woman shows and questionable boyfriends. But if I wanted to get through to her and convince her to leave with me, I'd have to catch myself before any reflexes of fakeness took over.

Summer pulled the cage back and revealed the meteorite. It was a chunk of marbled metal, a weathered depth charge of a ball.

Glowfolk approached her with trepidation, folding their ponchos beneath them as they sat on the floor by her feet.

She reached to pick up the meteorite.

A gasp passed between the Glowfolk as Gabriel sped towards her and pressed his hand on the meteorite, blocking her. The hand sizzled.

Nausea rose in my stomach as I watched his face flush with color. It showed how pale he'd been before.

Summer frowned at him. He was a good two feet taller than she was, but it didn't feel that way to look at them.

He cowered and reached into his pockets, pulling out a pair of nitrile gloves.

"Thank you," Summer said, accepting them.

He walked away, balling the sizzled hand into a fist. Rivulets of blood dribbled like rain down the impermeable plastic of his robe. He'd tried to hide it—therefore it was real.

Unless they wanted me to think that, and it was an invented display of power for a random inert object.

Her hands, now gloved, Summer lifted the ball. "Before the island, Patricia made plastic sculptures. She melted scraps together with a lighter." She balanced the stone in one hand and gestured to the plant flesh beneath the plinth.

I watched in awe as streams of light, which spread from the stone's housing, died. Colors faded, the light extinguished. The thicker vines that ran up the parapets constricted, withered and went clear.

The members held their breath as if they too were dormant, awaiting power restoration.

"She rowed herself out here each day to gather plastic. In the evenings, she returned to the streets of Southend and assembled her creations. She'd sit beside them and beg for money. And that's where I found her."

I looked at Joanna. She mouthed Summer's words, having surely heard them countless times before. And yet she was crying.

"I invited Patricia to a café," Summer continued, "but she didn't want to leave her sculptures. They were more than just a way for her to make money. I asked her what got her started with the plastic and she told me about her visions of weird creatures in kaleidoscopic dimensions. They spoke to her of mankind's wastefulness, demanded monuments of themselves and a temple in which to place them, to demonstrate our hubristic destruction. They spoke of a stone, falling from the sky, which would provide us with all that we needed to rid ourselves of our current ways of life." She held the meteorite in one hand and pressed a gloved finger to her chin in thought. "I'll never forget my first conversation with Patricia. Before we met, I was just a lonely divorcee, a middling GP. A truly contemptible and lowly individual, stagnating in life."

I talked about myself in my head like that, yet to hear

similar words about a stranger, I was convinced they were too harsh. How did that work?

"Now that Patricia has to store her energy for higher level activities, I see what a privilege our early time together was." She held the meteorite to her chest, clasping her hands together. "She took me to an abandoned building, where she'd kept her plastic replicas of the weird creatures. We took them to my garage. Together we made so many that I had to rent out a warehouse space, and that's when the press got involved. With the remaining followers we gathered from the extra attention, we made the island. We secured ourselves to its then-rudimentary floor, in our sleeping bags, with bungee cords and hooks."

Didn't sound at all likely, and yet here I was, floating on the very structure they built. If this island didn't exist, I definitely wouldn't have believed it could be made. Another Glow trick, transporting you to an unbelievable place to ease further mental stretches?

Summer held up the meteorite. "On the seventh day, we awoke to the smell of burning plastic. The stone had landed, strange plants flourishing from its surface. They filled with light and warmth. Channels of pure water ran through their veins and their spores cleansed the air."

If any of this was fake, it was still impressively elaborate.

She returned the meteorite to its socket. Light filled the plants once again. They hummed, their leaves, nodes and fronds jittering with excitement.

The kid in the baseball cap laughed and nudged his friends, who shushed him loudly.

Joanna stood up and walked over to him, whispering something in his ear.

"Look how our island," Summer continued, "powered by the stone, rewards us with its own life."

Veins pumped glowing fluid through them, gave life to the island's dayglo cathedral of buildings.

Summer smiled. "Gabriel will give a brief tour, then lunch —and that's it. Go home if you want."

I wasn't scared yet. But it was only Day One of Three, the maximum duration I could expect to stay out here, alive. Who knew what next awaited us?

CHAPTER 7

Gabriel stood us, the new arrivals, in the plaza's center. He would give us a tour and I had to leave Joanna behind for now.

He told us that the island's body had satellite-controlled rotors at four corners, just like the ones they'd used on deep sea drilling rigs in the past. The rotors kept the island in place, away from the surrounding wind farms and shipping routes.

He explained what we'd find down the first three of four alleyways: buildings, up to seven stories high, made from plastic bottles—over a hundred thousand in total—in mesh nets, covered in cement.

Along the first alley, he showed us the communal living space and showers, where strips of a cane-like plant glowed bright white across the ceiling.

The second alley led to the hairdresser's, the laundry rooms, clothing stores and store rooms of food, toiletries, clean blankets and medical supplies.

Down the third alley were rooms containing the generators used for power, the biodigesters that harvested methane from organic waste, the algae reactors that made the biodiesel and the tanks that collected potable water from open veins of the island's weird plants.

We stopped to marvel at Patricia's sculptures, dotted throughout each of the rooms: octopus-like creatures made of burnt plastic, lumpy meteorite-like rocks, Picasso-esque self-portraits.

The fishery was our last stop.

Barnacles crunched under our feet as we entered a humid, cuboidal room at the end of Alley Three. It smelled like a lobster pot parching in the sun. A strange outcrop of plastic that looked like a sink emerged from the floor. Plant tendrils broke through the wall and bathed their tips in its water like toeless foot-stumps dabbling in a wading pool.

Large circular hatches in the floor were open to the water beneath. They contained "bivalve molluscs, decapod crustaceans as well as pelagic and demersal fish"—whatever those were.

"Wait," I said, "you all still eat real fish?"

"Exactly," Gabriel said.

The teenagers audibly squirmed. Heath remained reticent. Corinne had looked on the verge of puking for the last hour or so anyway.

"I know what you're thinking," Gabriel continued. "Mercury, cancer, etcetera. Well, let me just use one of our roaches to prove you wrong."

He saw the look on my face.

"It's a type of fish."

He went to the cupboard and took out a net on the end of a long rod. Opening one of the hatches, he dipped the net in and retrieved a fish about the length of my forearm, green on its top half fading to silver at its bottom.

He ushered us to follow and took us to the plastic sink.

This was the closest I'd been to the plant. It looked like dry ice, white and friable, encased in a coating of clear gelatin.

Once he'd dropped the flapping fish in from a height, it swam around him in panicked circles. The water thickened and the fish slowed until it was stationary in the pool's center. Didn't they have to keep swimming to survive? Or was that just sharks? I didn't know. Either way, the water's surface was still, shimmering like thick resin. A humming reverberated through the pool and the floor itself shook.

I steadied myself. Gabriel placed a hand on me, urging me to pay attention.

The fish's mouth expanded to its limit. Grayish lumps emerged and migrated their way through the resin. Smaller lumps and threads shot out the fish's rear end as well. As they did, they shed their dirt, their mass. They were pieces of plastic, shattering and dissolving, moving towards the plant's tendrils. The plants absorbed the milky droplets of plastic that remained.

The vibration stopped. The tendrils grew new nodules at their tips. The resin became water again and the fish swam in its circles, much calmer than before.

"It's not just the fish." Gabriel cupped a handful of water from the pool and drank it. "The water's fresh."

How do you fake something like that?

Gabriel folded his arms with self-satisfaction. "This is the work we do. Salvaging plastic, healing fish, purifying water. Any questions?"

I had to snap out of it. Didn't want to miss a chance to sow discord through the island's otherwise ironclad indoctrination.

"Do I know you from somewhere?" I asked.

The teenagers whispered. Heath looked between us with detached curiosity.

Gabriel raised an eyebrow. "I don't talk about acting anymore and if you came out here just to—"

I held a hand up to his face. "Whoa, whoa. I didn't say 'acting.' I don't think I've seen you in anything."

He hesitated. "You sure?"

"Oh yeah. I'd remember too." I got closer to him. "I always wanted to be in films. Sadly it wasn't to be."

Not really. When as objective as I could be about my own attractiveness, I didn't think myself ugly—but that didn't mean I enjoyed the prospect of blowing up my image and asking thousands, maybe millions of strangers to look at it for the rest of time.

"Being in films isn't for most people," Gabriel said.

"But it was for you. Apparently."

"I—" He sighed. "I was fortunate. But now I'm doing something else."

I held my hands up. "Fine."

"I couldn't go back anyway," he continued. "I already sold my appearance."

"Huh?" This did take me by surprise. And was unfortunate. He'd been a real talent, not just a looker. Up there on the big screen was a human soul, feeling its way through authentic emotions. Not anymore.

"They can superimpose me in anything they want to," he added, his aggression subsiding. "I-I'm not supposed to talk about it."

"I assume you got paid for that, and donated the money to the Glow? And now you're not even allowed to—"

A cold hand gripped my elbow. It was Corinne. She looked to the floor and said only "Lily, Lily."

"Sorry," I said. "Sorry. Lunch, then?"

"When the tour is over, yes," Gabriel said.

"Is it over?"

The teenagers tittered.

He frowned. "Yes."

We filed back out of the room.

"Hey."

I turned to Gabriel. "Hm?"

"If not from my acting, where do you know me from?"

"Sorry," I said. "It's just a line."

"A line?"

"I was flirting with you. I'm sure that's banned. Forgive me. I'm still learning."

"If you go back—to the land, I mean—could you watch my films? The new ones?" He pushed a palm to his forehead. "Forget it. And please don't tell anyone I said that."

I lowered my voice. "I will. Watch them. If you want me to."

I couldn't imagine myself back on land now, not without Joanna. As for watching his new films—taking in the soulless AI performances that the film studio would brand by plastering Gabriel's appearance onto them—the notion broke my heart.

We stood staring at one another. Gabriel broke eye contact first and looked to the rest of the group, who waited for us at the end of the alley.

"We should get back," he said.

And there our tour ended, before we went to the fourth alley. But I didn't ask about it. I'd pushed enough for now.

Though beleaguered by the no doubt draining lifestyle of the island, there remained something like a glimmer of humanity left in Gabriel's eye, in his wistful yearning for the adoration of his too-soon-abandoned career. It seemed that, if ever removed from slave labor and returned to proper nutrition, his film star looks and attitude would return.

So. If I survived, could I take him with me?

———

Back in the plaza, Joanna and I sat together at the table.

Summer sat in the white plastic throne. It folded to her with the insidiousness of a flytrap's closing jaws.

Members handed out cutlery and Styrofoam plates.

41

From large plastic buckets, they doled out watery-looking fish meat, and some sort of white vegetable, in equal measure.

"Is that the plant?" I asked Joanna.

She nodded.

"I'm not eating that!"

"I eat it every day. It's fine." She saw the look on my face. "It takes longer than half a day to learn about our life out here. You'll just have to trust me."

Just have to trust her! Well, I didn't. Not her slow, measured words. Her practiced, pre-approved speech. Not the manic look in her overly wide eyes nor the slight grinding of her rear molars. Not my former glamourpuss sister's broken nails, brittle hair, sallow skin.

"You want to stay longer, don't you?" She said.

In the past, when she'd tried to introduce her latest terrible boyfriend to the family, thoughts of spending time with her got tainted by a vague sense of dread and regret, that it wouldn't be as fun as I was imagining it, or like it was before. Well, I carted a flurry of similar types around myself, and where all these early relationship attempts were concerned, Joanna had an excellent excuse for her poor taste: she may well have never been attracted to men.

The rest around the table ate rapturously.

Anyway, as I bit into the plant, which had the crunchy texture and bland taste of water chestnut, I thought about how the Glow was the worst partner of Joanna's that I'd ever met.

———

After lunch, members cleared the plates away and Summer asked us visitors to gather over by the harbor, where our bags were waiting.

Joanna and I walked over together.

"Okay folks," Summer said with the grating enthusiasm of a camp leader. "Melodie will head back to town now."

Cleverly phrased. Almost like Melodie was free to roam the shops rather than simply sit in that dodgy plastic powerboat and wait for new visitors or meager supplies.

"So," Summer continued, "unless you want to stay here overnight…"

The kid, who'd laughed during Summer's speech, now watched his two friends get in the boat. He made it seem like an extended goof to his friends, that he was going to outdo them in a contest of ironic dares by spending an extra day here—but I could tell when Joanna had gotten to someone.

"Hey." Joanna took me aside from the rest. "If you're gonna stay longer, you can sleep in my room. There's extra space, and it'll be like we're kids all over again."

Not quite.

Ella walked up behind her, wincing at her suggestion. When I caught her eye, a fake smile flicked onto her face.

Joanna scratched her neck. "Only if you're considering, you know—"

"Sure I am."

Heath and Corinne came up to me.

"I'm out," Corinne said.

On her site, I'd watched videos of her infiltrating neofascist gangs and testing out new designer drugs on herself while they were still legal. She had brought warlords to tears, but she was bailing on *this?*

She stood, frozen, but her eyes twitched around. "You can't feel that?"

I knew what she meant. My still-tense stomach muscles ached. But she hadn't even wanted me here in the first place. Maybe there was a reason she wanted me back off again that I hadn't thought of yet.

I shrugged weakly. "What else can I do?"

"The same thing you did with Gabriel. I saw what you

were up to. You know how to plant a seed of doubt and bail. Go to—to Joy. Tell her you're so glad she found a community that's doing important work and making her happy. Then leave. You've got to hope that's enough."

"Everything okay?" Ella said.

"My wife's leaving," Heath said.

"And you?"

"Not yet."

He looked at me. His kindly brown eyes had a glint of humor in them. He blinked slowly, as if to say, *everything will be okay*.

"Last chance, Lily," Corinne said to me.

"I appreciate your concern," I told her coldly.

She lowered her head, defeated and saddened, and got in the boat with the girls.

CHAPTER 8

After I had declined to join the others in the communal shower, Joanna took me down Alley one and up a bottle ladder to the very top of one of the towers that overlooked the plaza. There, we found a door constructed from broken plastic pallets with *JOY* spelled out in keyboard keys on the front. This was a privilege of "EOs", Exalted Ones, like herself.

She hinted that to earn the title, the room and the right to wear her EO tunic, she'd had to demonstrate her allegiance to the Glow in ways she was evidently proud of. But I abstained from further questioning. I didn't want to validate her sacrifice and I was also afraid to learn just what my sister was capable of.

Beyond her door was a first apartment-sized clear bulb, like blown glass. It had weathered poorly, with games consoles, pieces of plastic chair and power extension sockets used to plug the holes.

I planted my suitcase by the door and looked around. She had a writing desk with warped paper on it, some broken pencils and a pink plastic vase. On a fishing line duct-taped to the wall were hangers recovered from the sea. Some were plastic, some wooden and spotted with black mold. Floaty dresses, skirts and cardigans hung from them. She'd assembled a fairy light-like chain of glowing algae clumps on the wall and among them were laminated postcards of the sky and sea.

It was like a full-scale plastic diorama of her bedroom in our family home, but in place of a bed, she had four curved hammocks that emerged from the wall. Still, it was as if her taste in interior decoration had frozen the day she ran away.

"It's cute," I said. "I mean, it won't protect against a nuclear blast when the end of days comes."

Not a genuine threat—no more so than ever—but a common object of Glow paranoia. I cursed my nerves for the insensitive joke. As if Joanna was going to take my side and laugh at the Glow with me!

Instead she perked up. She walked up to me and grabbed my shoulders, mania in her eyes. "Well that's the thing," she said. "When they bomb, where are they gonna bomb?" Said with such confidence, as if we both knew "they" would bomb one day. Whoever "they" were.

I fell mute.

"They'll bomb the land of course," she said. "And there are always a handful of awake people here at any time. We'll see danger if there is one. We do emergency drills for it all the time. Gabriel can reconfigure the stabilizing motors and send us into open water in under three minutes."

I wasn't going to quiz her on that.

"You're safer here than anywhere else."

Jesus, I hoped not. What would it mean if that was true?

We went to opposite sides of the room so we could get changed into pajamas.

As I took my jacket off, I searched my pockets for my watch. Nothing. That handsy Glow member must have pickpocketed it upon my arrival.

Unless I had left it in the suitcase. I laid the case on the floor and unzipped it. Of what I remembered packing, my dry shampoo, books for Joanna and bag of kratom were missing.

There was a note inside. I turned to check that Joanna was still distracted by getting changed, and read:

Dear Visitor,

Thank you for your interest in the Glow. We are always looking for new recruits to help with our mission!

We operate with a strict no tolerance policy towards items of paraphernalia that are commonplace on land.

For your future reference, the following forbidden items were found in your personal belongings:

A list, with boxes beside each item, followed. Someone had ticked *outside literature, technology* and *alcohol/controlled substances.*

Should you leave the island, we will return these items to you, no harm done.

I should've expected as much. With no way of updating Henry, it meant he would soon come after me.

After I got changed, Joanna ushered me to one of the hammocks. I climbed in, the clear path to the floor down below giving me vertigo. We towered over the central plaza's quilt of weird mulch, a pink light pulsing across its surface. I tried to steady myself, the island rolling, pitching, heaving—all three, I assumed. Though I didn't know the difference.

Joanna giggled. "You okay?"

I pressed a palm to my forehead. "I'm getting lightheaded."

Joanna blew some hair out of her face. "It's the plants. They purify the air with oxygen. You're breathing what air used to be like. It was *this* clean."

"Wow."

She took off her poncho and hung it on a hanger. "I didn't know if you'd ever come."

"Sorry to separate you from your wife."

She sunk into a hammock and scratched her cheek on one shoulder. "She has other commitments on the island to keep her occupied. I-I'm used to it."

"Is *she*, though? She didn't look too pleased at the idea. And is it a problem that she knows we're sisters?"

She swung her legs back out the hammock and leaned, looking at me. "I know what you're doing. You're trying to shame me. So go on, let me have it. I'm with another woman."

I sat up to face her. "You think I'm mad because—" I scoffed. "I knew that about you. Plus it's the forties, Joanna. No one cares. Even I've had a frisson or two before."

She was shocked.

"I'm mad you didn't tell me you got married. For *starters*."

Her eyes flitted about as she searched her brain, recoloring her memories with new information.

"Please tell me that's not what this is all about."

Her expression changed back to indignation. "I assume by 'all this' you mean my life's work? No. You should know what it's about by now."

"Jojo—"

"It's Joy. Joy!"

She must have known I'd have no problem with her wife. Maybe others on the island had families that had legitimately cast them out. I'd hate to think it still happened, but it wasn't impossible.

Joanna needed a reason not to get in touch with us again. If I was right that she'd invented this flimsy excuse to keep herself away, it was promising. It meant I hadn't snubbed her in some more serious way—and that the lies she told herself to stay here had serious weaknesses in their foundation.

I got up, sat beside her and rubbed her back. "I'm glad you've found something that makes you this happy, that gives you so much purpose."

She leaned her head to one side. "That's kind of you. I know it isn't much. Summer says we need to get our numbers up before we can make real progress." She untied my hair and began to plait it loosely over my shoulder, an affectionate gesture trained into her subconscious. "How did you make it here?"

"What do you mean?"

"Mum couldn't even bathe you in the sink when we were kids."

"Huh." I thought of the morning, the haze of kratom, the bobbing sea. "I guess the thought of never seeing you again scared me even more."

She dropped my hair and lay down. "That's enough for one day."

Thank God. I've been "on" all day.

I went back to my hammock and tugged on my sleeves. The night's ocean breeze permeated the wall's gaps and coursed through my clothes.

I looked up at the dusky sky. Stars shone through the ceiling's opaque surface. I didn't know what time it was, but it seemed early for bed. Not like I was about to sleep anyway.

I looked over to Joanna. I wanted to take her by the hand and run. But she wasn't ready.

She sat up.

I closed my eyes

I heard her put on a robe, its frayed edges scratching against the floor.

She shuffled away and left the room.

I got up to watch where she went, but as I did, a headache took over, the room blurred and I passed out on the floor.

CHAPTER 9

"Congratulations!" Joanna said.

I opened my eyes to the stinging sun's cool, cloud-filtered light.

She was already dressed in her full ceremonial gear. "You made it to day two." Her pitch grated my nerves. It was the same one she'd used as a teen when I'd stumble down to breakfast with her and Mum, poorly disguising a hangover.

I was in the hammock again. My suitcase was upright and zipped up.

Last night—was it kratom withdrawal? Fatigue? Gin catching up with me? Something the Glow did?

I'd been conducting a cruel experiment on myself and couldn't parse out which of the bad things happening to me was doing what. And besides, I had to remember—given the Glow's capacity for reprogramming people—this "Joy" woman, who took the shape of my sister, could be anything but. Even if it pained me to suspect her.

"Last night," I said to her. "I swear—"

"We need to go to the plaza straight away, before anyone knows you stayed here."

Oh boy, more confusing layers of secrecy.

She clapped her hands. "Up, up!"

I tugged at her robe. "I need to talk to you. Now."

She went over to the entrance hatch and climbed down the ladder.

I quickly got into a change of clothes and followed.

———

The plaza was unbearably bright. Water had sloshed over it during the night, turning it into a massive sun mirror. Evenly spaced yoga mats broke up the reflections. They covered most of the free area. The plants twisted up between them and expand, fuzzing with new growths. The horizon rose and fell with the island's motion upon the murky sea.

Summer stood on the podium in front of all the Glowfolk. They surrounded her in an evenly spaced grid, a carpet of people about twenty long and ten wide.

"Glad you could join us, Lily," Summer said.

A titter spread across the group. They could do better than that, surely, but I wasn't about to bring it on my own head.

"You're forgiven," she added, pressing her palms together. "The rhythms of all of us are synced, but it's not uncommon for newbies to lag."

"At least I'm not the last arrival."

Oh. The looks on their faces. You didn't answer back to the leader. Well, *they* didn't.

"Where are Heath and that other kid?"

"That's right." Summer looked across the group. "We lost two faces last night. Michael—'the kid'—didn't possess the sea legs necessary to help save the world."

I flinched once again at the group's forced laughter.

"He had second thoughts, so we made a special trip to ship him back to the land. No harm done. All are welcome to leave whenever."

"Huh," I said.

"We had to send Heath packing too. We found cameras set up in the communal bedrooms."

The Glowfolk gasped.

"He was a reporter."

Exaggerated murmurs, mournful wails.

I didn't know if Heath would've set up cameras, but I did believe the Glow would find an excuse to kick a journalist out. As for the kid, sure, maybe the apparent ironic joke of staying here wore thin during the night and he panicked. That they had left was plausible. As it would be if the Glow had done something to them and wanted to cover it up.

"You didn't know about Heath's profession, did you, Lily?"

An eager middle-aged woman close to the group's front jumped up and down, raising her arm.

"Yes, Rachel?"

"Did he compromise us?"

"Cameras or no, it makes no difference. The plants don't allow it."

"Right," the woman said, satisfied with this answer. But what the hell did it mean?

"Lily." Summer looked right at me again, keen for me to acknowledge that she knew my name.

"Yes, Summer," I said back.

"You're in time for a wellbeing session with Ella."

I grimaced. "It's not private, is it?"

The group laughed.

Ella stood beside the podium, smirking and shaking her head.

Joanna nudged me with an elbow. "I'm so excited for you to see what she does!"

I placed a hand on hers, turned to her and smiled. She wanted me to be a part of this. That was a good sign. It amused me to picture both of us living in an apartment together in the future, no longer separable, all the significance of this time together hitting Joanna in increments. Maybe over morning tea, while we both read the news on our devices, she'd slap herself on the forehead and say, "*You* were humoring *me* that day!"

If that's what I wanted, there was work to do.

Ella took to the stage. "Let's get started."

"With what?" I asked Joanna.

"The dance."

I froze. "How long are we going to dance for?"

"I'm not sure. I only know that when I get started, I usually don't want to stop." She ushered me towards a mat. "You'll enjoy it."

Glow aside, group activities were not my thing—though they'd always been Joanna's. I thought of an early Club Med holiday, how she'd clung to my side, following me into the nine-to-twelve-year-olds group, though she wasn't old enough, crying when they wouldn't let her make a kite with me.

"Okay everyone, blindfolds out."

Each member took from their robe what looked like a pad made from layers of plastic bags sewn together, with an elastic cord at both ends. They covered their eyes with them.

"I've got yours here." Joanna removed two of the same masks from her pocket.

I just had to get through this. Then I could get back to my amateur, low-res cult-deprogramming attempt.

I took the mask from her and secured it over my eyes.

"Phase one," Ella said. "Jump up and down."

I had a peek at everyone else. They jumped without coordination, like children in the throes of a tantrum.

I could muster that much. I hopped from foot to foot and flailed my arms in a loose jumping jack motion.

We did this until I almost couldn't anymore, my head

aching, hamstrings cramping. I always said the most things I didn't mean and agreed to the most stuff I didn't want to do when I was tired. I had to assume that was the exercise's purpose, and reminded myself to remain vigilant.

"Phase two. Breathing. Listen to me and find the breath within yourself."

She panted raggedly and the group followed her command, reaching astounding volume. Anytime anything external—some meditation app or yoga video, say— threatened to control my breathing, the very thought gave me anxiety. It was my body, my lungs—surely any suggestion wasn't healthy, let alone the shallow panting of a dog in a hot car that Summer now performed.

I got lightheaded again. Spots popped across my vision, even with my eyes closed.

"Stay in your places for phase three, everyone! This isn't a contact sport."

"This is my favorite!" a man screamed.

The rest whooped with joy.

"Now go crazy!"

I felt this one beneath me. The rumbling, feet stamping, bodies rolling on the wet floor. Aching sobs, outraged screaming.

Once the fear subsided, and I remembered they couldn't see me, I joined in. I windmilled my arms, spun around, screamed. I gasped in the fresh air, so unaccustomed to it that it got me high.

The floor tilted beneath me. With each jump, I didn't know whether to trust that it would still be there. My feet never landed when I expected them to, and the texture of mushy plastic, moss and seawater felt different each time. As I jumped, I spent more time in the air than the jump before. I half-expected to take off into the sky. Instead, I felt something constricting my waist and I shrunk within myself.

"You're a child!" she said. "Go to your favorite place!"

The spots in the darkness expanded, images of my childhood with Joanna rushing across my vision. I saw the forest of our youth, reeds on the bank as tall as I was, our welly boots sinking in the mud. Ripples spread across the pond where hungry fish mouths broke the water's still surface.

"Lily!"

It was Ella, calling me.

I reached for the mask to see where she was, but she tutted, and I felt her hand press the mask to my face.

"Concentrate now," she said. "Stay where you are. Describe it to me."

I mentioned the reeds, the mud, the pond. I refrained from telling her about the fear, the panic clutching my chest, the dread seeping through my entire body.

"I can see it," Ella said. "Can you see it, group?"

"Yes," they said in unison. It rang through my body like a wall of comfort. As if a community was there with me that day.

"How old are you?" She asked.

"Twelve, I guess."

"You guess?"

"I'm twelve."

"Who's there with you?"

"Our dogs. Two border collies." Max and Benjamin, two fluffy and muddy best friends.

"Are you sure?"

With her words, the dogs disappeared again. "No. They've run ahead without me."

"That's right, they have."

Did she know, or was she somehow making it so?

"So I'll ask again," she said. "Who's there with you?"

"My sister." Little blonde Joanna in her blue checkered duffle coat, splashing in the puddles.

"Look again."

56

Just puddles. Just mud. "Nobody."

"Look again."

"A man." Herringbone slacks, the pungent scent of cigars.

"Describe him."

"He's wearing a yellow raincoat and a matching cap. It's like something a child would wear. And the ground is wet, but it hasn't been raining. The cap hides his face."

Ella was silent now. I was off, the words running away from me. Some long-forgotten experience—no, a long-repressed trauma—now spilling out of me, for the whole group to hear. How?

"He asks me for directions to a campsite. I say I don't know." More than I was allowed to say to strangers. "He has a map under his arm. He wants me to point out where." As if I would know! "But the map is bulky like it's wrapped around something."

"Go on."

"He holds it out to me. I turn away and he seizes my arm." Like I was back there again, his thick fingers like a vice squeezing my little bones. Like running in a dream without moving. "He pulls me up."

The constriction around my waist returned.

"I'm kicking and screaming."

But I couldn't reach the ground's safety. I flailed in the air, helpless, drowning in the nightmare of it.

"Stay there, Lily. Stay there."

"Until—"

"Yes?"

"He's screaming too." Release. In my memory, I fell to the floor again. I felt the cool wet mud soaking into my favorite red corduroy dungarees. "He drops me. My sister, she digs her teeth into his ankle. He runs away. My sister holds her mouth. It's bleeding. She left two front baby teeth in the man's leg."

When they arrested the Rendlesham Ripper, they found

those teeth in a locket around his neck—along with many others that weren't Joanna's.

And there it was, the reason I owed it to my sister to seek her out.

CHAPTER 10

Someone shook my arm. I tried to move it, but couldn't. My eyes had shut tight and my body had curled into fetal position. I was catatonic.

I unfroze, gasped for air. I clawed my hands over my ears, palms pressed flat against them. It was a reaction to the screaming. It was so loud. Who was doing it? When would it stop?

Arms tugged at me. They wrenched the hands from my ears and took the mask off my face. My eyes opened and I saw a looming circle of Glowfolk around me, looking down on me with pity.

I was the one screaming. Once I realized this, I could stop.

"Get up," Ella said.

I stood and faced her.

"That's why you're here, isn't it? To save someone, like you were once saved."

"I-I guess so."

"You guess so?"

A pit of something like decades-old shame welled up in my stomach. The Ripper—my first and fortunately rare reminder that no one is ever safe. Joanna's act is my first lesson that there is no guarantee in life but our own actions.

It led me to the island. It taught me not to trust others, only myself.

Ella placed a hand on my shoulder. "I was there with you. I saw what you saw. You haven't moved past the memory because your twelve-year-old self learned the wrong message from it. Which was?"

"One day I need to save the person that saved me."

She smiled. "You came here to save your sister."

Rumors flew across the group:

"Sister!"

"Is her sister here?"

"Who is it?"

"Joy, the EO."

"They were talking together yesterday."

"Hey!" Ella motioned for the others to shush. She looked to me again. "Joy's not the one you need to save. But, stay. Work with us. Save others. Starting with yourself."

She embraced me, pressing my head against hers, swaying me from side to side with her body.

I took in her scent. Jasmine. I released all my muscles at once.

As if they knew I'd do that, the Glowfolk rushed in to take my weight, swaying me to the rhythm of Ella's movements.

"Tell us what you feel," someone said.

"Yeah, Lily! Share with us? Please?"

What did it mean that they knew about Joanna now? And what did I think about the memory, if that's what it was?

Everything went too fast. The group's attention exerted a pressure on me to perform to their satisfaction. And I still hadn't eaten.

I broke down, tears gushing down my face. My arms rushed out, independent from me, and gripped Ella.

When my arms fell at my side again, all of them released me and stood back, forming a concentrated circle.

"Why didn't you warn me?" I said.

"You wouldn't have done it otherwise," Ella said.

Paternalistic bullshit. I hadn't even subscribed yet and already they were making decisions for me.

Though I did feel something like—well, a glow inside. Like the high I got those few dry Januarys that I managed to abstain from drinking. Time would tell if it really was the catharsis it seemed to be.

"Lily," Ella continued, "if you hadn't gone through this, they would have ordered me to send you home."

The old "above my pay grade, mate" excuse. They probably call it "above my trophic level" or some shit out here.

"Neither of us want that," Ella added.

So apparently she was psychic as well as deeply invasive.

"We all went through it." It was Gabriel's soothing voice behind me. "I ran away from home as a kid. During my first session I saw it from my mother's perspective. It was devastating."

"Summer did it for me back on land," Ella said. "In my vision, I was my own friend and, in this role, I had to watch a condensed version of my drug and drink years. The process releases traumas in order of urgency."

It would've felt good that they shared their own struggles —if I had any reason to believe them. Without proof, I just felt ashamed by my own warped memories.

"Don't you feel good now?" Gabriel said. Why was he being kind to me? Did he like me or just the attention I gave him? If I couldn't figure that out about regular, land-based men, what hope did I have of decoding him?

"May I be excused for a moment?" I said.

The group reacted with stiffness. They seemed to think I'd melt right into them. It pleased me to subvert. I didn't want any involvement in things going their way.

"Sure," Ella said.

I nodded and headed towards Joanna's room. It surely

wasn't great that they knew who my sister was. Either way, I no longer had a reason to hide it.

I felt them beneath me in the plaza. Their confusion, their rigidity.

None of them could leave an activity at will—but they had to convince me I could, at any time, if they wanted me to join.

CHAPTER 11

I savored my time alone in Joanna's room, sitting in a hammock, drying my face on a t-shirt.

Was there a mirror somewhere? I hadn't brought one.

I searched Joanna's desk. Something poked out beneath her vase. They were photos of us together at some London nightclub.

And I thought she didn't think of me at all. It was worse that she did. She knew the sacrifice she'd made, but she thought it was worth it.

No! I couldn't think like this. I had to stay focused.

I looked down at the plaza. Everyone's head had turned my way. When I met their eyes through the cellophane window, grins shot across their faces instantly. I grinned back and came back down.

We were going to eat soon. I still didn't know if there was a reason I passed out when Joanna left last night, but maybe it was what they fed me.

I ducked into the store room on my way back down the alley and stole an unlabeled can to put in my jacket. Maybe that was better than what they were about to serve us.

I sat beside Joanna at the day's one meal.

The faces around the table were different. I'd estimate that only a third of the people I'd seen on the island could fit round it at once. I wasn't sure that meant the others were eating elsewhere.

I stared at the plate before me—the same overboiled fish meat and bland, alien vegetable—and kept wiping my face as new tears emerged. Around me was the animal sound of others devouring their food.

"Stop crying, would you?" Joanna said. "It isn't a big deal. I expected more from you."

"I notice you're not eating, Lily," Summer said.

"No need to worry," I said. "I'm still adjusting to the island's motion. B-But I won't let that stop me being here."

"It isn't that our offering displeases you, then?"

Joanna let out a deep breath, as if trying to calm herself because of my insult.

"Not at all."

"Eat, then," Ella said from the other end of the table.

"Maybe there's something else we can make for you?" Gabriel suggested, looking at the other members.

"Thank you, but no. Please. No special treatment."

"So enjoy," Summer said. It was a command.

I took the plastic knife and fork and sliced a piece of the plant, raising it slowly to my mouth.

"Look!" Joanna said. "New arrivals."

I put the fork down.

"I almost forgot," Summer said. "Melodie's late today. I'll be interested to learn why. Lily, come with us. You'll have to learn how to greet the new arrivals."

Glowfolk scurried away from the table, off to collect their sparklers.

We gathered over by the harbor.

The two girls from yesterday got out the boat. Melodie remained at the back, by the motor, looking ashamed. Waif that she was, there was no way she could've prevented them from getting on the boat.

"Where is he?" said the taller one.

"Welcome," Ella said, ignoring the question.

"Don't pretend like you don't know," the shorter one said.

Summer approached them. "Hello again, girls. Your friend left last night. You haven't seen him yet?"

What was going on? I wanted to stay and find out, but this was my chance to do something about the food. I retreated from the group that had gathered, everyone from the island, and went back to the table. I chopped up my food and redistributed it onto the other plates.

I'd stay at the table and pretend I'd eaten alone. Hopefully I was just paranoid and wouldn't have to do this again in future, or else they'd get suspicious.

Soon the crowd returned to the table.

"Lily?" Summer said. "The girls left again."

"Thanks for letting me know." I stood to talk to her. "I get nervous when people watch me eat. I'm sure I'll get used to it."

She looked at my plate, then back at me. "Fine."

———

That afternoon was my first experience of Summer's "discourse." Can someone give a discourse by themselves?

Apparently so. She sat on the throne as purple tentacles waved loosely around her, at least twenty, all of varying lengths and shades. Their movement was menacing, like Medusa's hair. They remained in constant motion as if anticipating an attack.

Summer spoke about the eternal nature of Truth—I could hear her capitalizing the word in her head. Not to say I understood the rhetoric. It sounded like a meaningless barrage of simple sentences spoken at a forcedly slow pace to introduce false reverence. I didn't think the others got it either. But their glazed eyes and rictus-ridden faces beamed at her, daffodils turning to their sun.

I'd almost ended up in a situation like this once before. When I was just an intern at the office, one of the accountants told me he was in a band and invited me to their gig that evening. "Cute, stable job and creatively inclined" wasn't usually my type—I preferred punishing myself with the meaningless challenge of less well-put-together men—but when I went home that evening, I messaged him to say I'd be there, and prepared some "I'm enjoying this" faces in the mirror in case the band wasn't any good.

The address he'd given me, I discovered when I showed up, was a church. When I went inside, I saw a group of teenagers on stage with keyboards, guitars and a drum set singing "God is awesome" over and over. My "date" was in the audience, his arms and theirs flowing with the music like seaweed in a wave.

I turned to leave, but he noticed and ran up to me. He shamed me, while smiling, for not giving the event a chance.

His behavior infuriated me beyond my standard first-date-turned-out-to-be-asshole peak. I couldn't make sense of it at the time, though I worked it out later. It was the insult that, without his manipulation, I wouldn't have been open-minded enough to attend of my own volition.

I'd always associate similar invitations in future with his trick. I told myself, for better or worse, that if any such organization had a secret worth knowing, it would be self-evident. They wouldn't have to use such tactics.

Which isn't to say that those tactics stopped working on me. Those inclined to use them dedicate so much energy to their development that they're always at least one step ahead. I'd just crossed my fingers that I'd catch the trick and bail in time.

After sitting cross-legged for hours, my groin muscles ached. And when had my back muscles gotten so weak?

When the discourse ended, we stood back up. Melodie asked if Joanna, Ella and I wanted to join her and her friends to play board games. "We're getting sick of playing amongst ourselves." She leaned in. "Maybe the newbie can beat Brandon!"

"No thanks," I said.

Melodie smiled weakly. "Another time, then."

She walked away, leaving Joanna, Ella and me standing together.

I looked to Joanna. "Back to your room, sis?"

"It's fine," Ella said to Joanna, affectionately smoothing her hair. "We'll catch up eventually."

"Come on, then." Joanna grabbed my elbow and whisked me away.

———

"What was that all about?" Joanna said.

We were back in her room, getting changed into pajamas.

"I need some help here," I said. "Which part?"

"Well, how about the way you spoke to Melodie?"

I tried to process everything that had happened. "Surely that's not what's bothering you? I haven't seen you in years. I didn't even know you were still alive." *I may never see you again.* "I don't want to spend what little time we have together playing board games with someone else."

"We're all equal here. You don't have the right to demand special time with any one of us."

"Okay."

She pulled on her hair, close to the root. "You came all the way out here just to persecute me again!"

"Again? Y-You didn't see it that way. That's not true."

I sat in the discomfort for a moment, wondering whether

her words really didn't ring true or if I simply wouldn't accept them.

No. They didn't sound like the Joanna I remembered.

I stabbed at a guess. "That ritual I was in this morning. Ella only pays that much attention to the newbies, doesn't she?"

Her eyes rolled around. She was searching for the next line in the script the Glow had installed in her mind.

"Does the process still work as well for you as it did for me this morning?"

She looked back at me, grimacing, straining to keep me out.

"Has your time here gotten better or worse?"

No! The question was too transparent. My agenda had leaked.

She climbed into the hammock and looked away from me. "I've kept you safe so far. My own courtesy to you. I guess I still had—a fondness for you that I've failed to let go of. Even as an EO, I always have more to learn."

Whatever glow I'd felt in her presence dimmed back to a familiar numbness.

"You think it's some tragedy that we never hang out." She turned back to me. "You're alone there. Because you've been living life 'on rails.' If anyone ever asked me if I had family on land I said, 'An alcoholic disappointment of a mother and a spineless sister. The sister she's nearing thirty now, settling down with the wrong man, thinking about having kids she doesn't want so she can give up on the career she didn't have in her to develop. All the while feeling sorry for me! Truly having it all."

I shut my eyes tightly. "I would slap you in the face right now. But things didn't go so well for me last time I did that to someone."

I wished I hadn't even said it. But only saying it, and not doing it, took the summation of my restraint.

She turned away again. "Running away from you is the kindest thing I could've done. On top of all I've accomplished since, it gave you the excuse you needed to become the massive failure we always knew you were."

I didn't have it in me to cry anymore. I hardly had any energy left at all.

"This is your last night in my room. And you should leave tomorrow."

My heart filled with a weird leaden peace.

In the best case, I'd thought, I would've left with Joanna and never parted from her again. Instead, I got confirmation that that would never be possible. Which was something. Disappointing, but still worth it. At least I hoped I would conclude that in years to come.

I lay back, done for the day. For the year, maybe. Once I got off the island, I'd process all my feelings. I was too worn out to do it now, and everything was going by so quickly, an assault on my emotions.

Here was something else I couldn't work out: I remembered reading in the news that when they'd arrested the Rendlesham Ripper, they found teeth in a locket around his neck. But where did I get the idea that Joanna's were in there too?

Had Ella pushed me in that direction, irritated that I had disturbed her ecosystem, stolen her possession away?

"Joanna?" I whispered. "Joy, I mean. Joy?"

She didn't reply.

I couldn't sleep. Too confused, too hungry, half-expecting Henry to show up, as he'd promised, to fire a gun in the air and order immediate evacuation.

And I still hadn't showered.

I leaned down to the floor and pulled up my jacket where I'd left it, taking out the can. I held it up to the sun's dying light. What a shame it would be to open it now, given the many different treats I'd hoped to find within it over the afternoon.

I was about to tug on the ring pull, but then I noticed something.

I turned the lid. Close to one edge, there was a pin prick, light bending around it like a black hole.

I pull the ring back. The can didn't make the same satisfying *shuck* sound it usually did. The seal had been compromised. They were injecting the food with *something*, then.

I peeled back the lid out of curiosity anyway. Inside was some sort of meat gelatin. Dog food, maybe. I wouldn't be surprised.

Joanna stirred.

I placed the can on the floor, covered it with my jacket then lay back down and closed my eyes.

She walked over to me. Through my eyelids, I saw the shadow of her hand waving over me.

She left, just like she had last night.

With no sign that I would pass out again, I followed.

CHAPTER 12

By the time I'd reached the bottom of the ladder, Joanna had vanished.

I headed to the plaza in search of her. Its plants softly glowed its range of purples and pinks, shadows of fronds waving up across the walls, through the thin evening mist. It was like being in an underwater exhibit at an aquarium. I wish I could've sat and enjoyed it.

The sky hadn't yet turned to complete darkness. A dim red on the horizon lit the world in all directions.

There was no one around, but I could hear something whirring. As I sneaked across the plaza, I realized that it came from the last alley, behind the chicken wire.

I vaulted over the gate and followed the sound.

There was a cement building at the end of the walkway, with a metal door. I walked to it and entered.

Inside, it was bright, with a grime-laden floor. Dusty plastic bottles, without labels, lined a set of shelves by the wall. A collection of immaculate plastic pallets lay beside them, with a stack of sandwich bags on top.

I took one of the bags, crouched down and tugged at a glowing sprig. I swore I heard it squeal as I pulled it from the floor's plastic, its many roots emerging where they'd grown down the pores. I sealed it in the bag and put it in my pocket, shuddering as I felt it wriggle.

When I left tomorrow, someone would be keen to sample it.

A labyrinth of pipes snaked over the wall. A tall metal cylinder, painted army green, vibrated in the room's center. Gauges and dials covered its surface. A slender pipe pointed towards a large collecting vessel, a clear liquid dripping from its tip.

I looked at the tags on some of the other pipes. With arrows, they indicated the direction of flow, and read *seawater, freshwater, brine, air supply*. The freshwater collected in the vessel. It was an evaporator.

Didn't the plants provide all the freshwater they needed?

On the other side of the room was a round orange generator, a black cable running to the evaporator. A jerry can of diesel sat beside it.

Why do that if the plants provided all the energy they needed?

Sustainable my ass!

"Oh, but the congregation is too big now. We need to resort to these temporary measures while the plants grow," they'd say.

No need to quiz them on it, I could hear the answers already. I could gaslight myself and save them the bother— which was probably an intended effect of their rhetoric.

I went to the shelves and picked up one of the bottles. Did they contain the evaporator's freshwater? I looked at the bottle more closely. Its seal wasn't broken. Maybe they'd been taken straight from the supermarket. Would they even reuse these bottles, or claim to have scavenged them from the sea, turning them into construction materials?

I heard footsteps down the alley.

I hid under a tarp.

It was Gabriel, carrying a clipboard under his arm. On his

head he wore a visor that directed purple light onto his face and body. UV light, looked like.

Survival reflexes kicked in in the weirdest way. I slowly purged the air from my lungs, muscles tightening, making myself small and willing myself invisible. I tensed so hard it hurt and wanted so badly to gasp for air.

How is this helping? I asked my body to no avail.

What an idiot I'd been, trying to gain his allegiance earlier. If he caught me, I'd learn just how little this place cared about my wellbeing.

To say the least, I thought as my imagination ran riot.

He checked the gauge and logged its numbers on a clipboard. On his way back out, he looked at the bottle I'd touched and turned it around.

Then he left.

And once I heard him pace off to a reasonable distance, I started breathing again.

———

My close encounter with Gabriel hadn't deterred my investigations. This remained my only chance to find out more about the Glow's operations, and what I'd discovered so far just further spurred me on.

Further down the alley, I discovered something like a lost and found room.

A stack of clothing filled one corner, a half-pyramid running from floor to ceiling. I looked across the myriad different items: nothing like you could find in the store rooms in Alley One. Must've been surrendered by former selves, or brought in by outsiders.

Yes, that was it. There was that kid's gold-embroidered jacket.

They said he'd left in the night—but not before ditching his jacket here, apparently. Maybe he was still here and they kept the identity of new members secret for some reason? That he was in some training facility I hadn't yet discovered, dancing around in a plastic smock, having relinquished his material possessions?

Wishful thinking of the worst order.

As unpleasant as it might have been for the kid to join the Glow's ranks, what I feared had happened to him was far worse. I didn't want to think about it without some further confirmation, but the sight of his jacket caused me to perspire with dread. There was no unknowing it.

In a bucket in the corner was a stack of phones, watches and e-glasses. Gabber jaw dials, like black buttons, were scattered throughout. Disallowing them on the island was a new policy, then. But how did you get them out without surgery, and why?

I went through each of the devices: no battery, needed password, no SIM card.

There was mine! I recognized the scratches on my watch's face.

I turned it back on and tried to call Henry. No signal. "The plants don't allow it," Summer had said. Signal blockers were a more likely alternative.

From the plaza came the sound of a man screaming, a weird unholy howl. It was surely my cue to go find out the next horrific, unforgettable thing about the Glow. My feet understandably kept me rooted to the floor where I stood, as if through some weird magnetic force. But I overcame it, step by step, leaving the room and creeping back up the alley toward the sound.

———

Back in the plaza, the dozen or so EOs had assembled in a circle. They were naked but for clear plastic raincoats. Barefoot, they hopped from side to side, jackets crinkling as they did so. They waved their arms back and forth in the air. In their hands were clumps of plant flesh, pulsing the infected yellow, pink and red of a suppurating wound. The pulse matched the rhythm of their stamping feet.

They made weird huffing sounds, an unintentional throat-singing. The ground squished beneath their feet. The floor was spongier than before.

In the center of the dance was the throne. Whoever sat there was the source of the screaming.

As I crept further along the wall, I saw that it was Heath. They'd stripped him to his underwear. Plastic tentacles secured him to the throne. On his chest and stomach were several bite marks, fresh blood trickling down his flesh. His jaw flapped open and closed, but he didn't make any more sounds. Plant pulp glowed on his lips—a rushed dose of drug to stifle his next attempts to scream.

I looked back at the EOs and winced. Their mouths were bloody.

The lights of the plants snuffed out, leaving the EOs nothing but shadows. They snarled and pounced on Heath, the throne toppling backwards.

The swarm of them surrounded Heath. Their arms worked frantically, cracks and rips emanating from their cluster. Heath was just a corpse now, a meaty, larva-like lump on the ground.

The floor glowed again. In the island's phosphorescent night lights, a sticky puddle bubbled. It trained into the floor like a whitecap sighing back into the sea.

Joanna got up, blood still wet in her hair, shimmering in the moonlight. She looked right at me—but her eyes couldn't see.

The floor made spotlights beneath each of the EOs. As the circles of lights moved along the floor, the EOs followed, walking backwards into their respective alleyways.

After some minutes, I sneaked back across the plaza, to

the bottle ladder leading to Joanna's room. She'd gone somewhere else.

Now I knew what she meant by her room keeping me safe.

Hours later, I heard someone climbing up the ladder.

I closed my eyes.

Joanna sighed. I could tell it was her. She stroked my hair with affection, then returned to her hammock.

How badly I wanted—what, to return the love? To reach out to her and tell her it would all be okay?

No. Whatever that was wasn't—my sister.

The Joanna I knew was gone forever.

CHAPTER 13

"**S**leep well?"

I hadn't slept at all. My face was cold and dry in that way it was when I'd been anxious for a long time, the blood drawn from the surface to protect my core, skin left to its own devices to flake and break out as a result.

I winced. My eyes were dry too. I could feel puffiness beneath them.

I sat up and couldn't see anyone in the room with me.

"Look down."

I scurried over to the voice's source. Through the window I saw Summer, in front of all the Glowfolk, looking up at me.

I climbed into the hammock to dress myself, so they couldn't see, pulling clothing out my suitcase from the floor.

When I went down the bottle ladder, Joanna was among the waiting crowd. Good. Maybe she didn't want me here—and I sure didn't want to be here any longer—but she wouldn't let anything terrible befall me in the meantime. Surely.

"Good morning, Summer," I said. "I hope I didn't delay today's proceedings."

"Oh there's no hurry for what comes next," she said.

The group rushed me and carted me up by my arms and legs.

"No!" I thrashed around, but couldn't see anything but a blinding blanket of white clouds. The sides of an alley came into view as they continued to carry me. And then I smelled the fishery.

A hatch creaked open. They whipped me in by my legs. I caught a glimpse of some splashing roaches just before I broke the surface of their pool.

I went into lizard brain-mode, thrashing around, trying to stay afloat and find something to hold onto, maybe to scrabble back up. The sides of the pool, I discovered, were smooth plastic, without a single imperfection I could grip onto. Even as I scratched at it, my fingers slid back off. I tried to reach out and prop myself up by holding onto opposite sides of the pool, but it was too wide.

"We're very clear on our rules, Lily," Summer said.

I kept myself afloat, trying to swim in the center, though I didn't know how. I dipped beneath the surface, my feet reaching down to find the pool's bottom, but it was too deep for me to stand on and keep my head above water. I held my breath, dropped to the bottom and kicked off the base to resurface and breathe again.

"You entered a restricted area last night."

"I can't swim!" I shouted.

"Y-You hear that?" It was Gabriel. "She's scaring my fish."

As he said that I felt them thrashing around me, heads bumping into my torso, tails and fins flapping against my hands.

"Come on." That was Ella. "She's not doing so badly. How do you expect her to learn otherwise?"

Other Glowfolk chimed in. "Why is she freaking out? It's just water. If she's serious about being here, it has to stop bothering her this much."

"Mhm I agree."

"It's hardly torture."

When I looked up and cleared the hair from my face, I tried to see who was up there, staring down at me.

Summer had gone. Gabriel looked at me with pity, Ella with detached curiosity, and Joanna with pure disdain.

And then they all left.

Cold. It was so cold. Maybe I could stay warm by moving in circles, keep burning energy. But the pool wasn't big enough for that. All of this had to be by design.

So I would drown here, among the roaches.

Someone tugged on my jacket, held me above water. "Shh shh shhh. You're doing great, Lily." That sounded like Melodie. But she held me from behind, so I couldn't be sure. "I know it doesn't seem like it right now, but this is good for you. I can't let them see me helping you. But use this as a chance to calm down."

I tried to lengthen and deepen my breaths. It took a while, but she held me there as I did.

"That's good. You're okay. You're going to be okay. You're going to come out of this stronger."

I couldn't speak, but I reached up and held her arm to show my appreciation.

"I have to go now. But you can do this."

In response, I wailed. Tears formed and washed away in the pool.

"Oh hey," I heard Melodie say to someone as she left. "Gabriel had me worried about the fish. Just wanted to check that they were okay."

"I'll remember that," said the man who'd discovered her there.

So I would stay here and suffer a while and get back out to find—what?

I slowed my strokes, my arms and legs coming to a stop. The weight of my wet clothes dragged me down.

I closed my eyes, breathed out, and dropped to the bottom.

Something constricted around my waist, around my arms. Seaweed, plastic garbage? I struggled against it, screaming out a last bubble.

I struggled, but whatever it was tightened further, pinning my arms in a cross over my chest.

Something pulled me up. I emerged from the water, hoisted up and out the hatch, back onto the plastic floor.

"Hooray!"

The Glowfolk had returned. I turned and fell on my chest, panting, to see five or six of them holding fishing rods, the wires wrapped around me.

A second wave of them lifted me to my knees and covered me with towels that they pressed on me.

"You did it."

"We're so proud of you."

"I knew you were made for this as soon as you arrived."

"You're definitely one of us now."

"Thank you for proving yourself to us. We won't forget, Lily."

The cheer in their voice gave no indication that they'd left me here to die.

I slumped back down on my side, shivering, jaw chattering.

"Well done, Lily," Summer said.

I held out my arms and the Glowfolk lifted me up, still holding the towels onto me, rubbing my hair with them.

"Bring her out for the surprise!"

Gabriel rushed over to me. "It's a good one this time," he said.

I couldn't even look at him.

CHAPTER 14

The Glowfolk had assembled around the stone outside, serene looks on all their faces. I thought I knew what was coming next.

Summer moved into position and placed her hand on the polygonal case.

I looked between her and the crowd. Joanna, Ella and Gabriel were at the front of them. I knew hardly any of these people still, yet all of them looked at me now with overly familiar grins on their faces, a kindness in their expressions, nodding their heads. Some of them cheered and whistled.

A young woman at the front sobbed aggressively and fell to her feet, shaking. Members on either side of her helped her up. "We're getting a new one," she said. "I can feel it!"

"Congratulations," Summer said. "The induction is over. You're free to join now."

"That's all it took, huh?" I said, coughing. My lips stung, drying out now that I'd returned to the light.

Ella tutted. "Did Joy never tell you what she went through to become Exalted?"

Joanna didn't look at me. She stared straight ahead, an empty vessel.

"One thing at a time!" Summer called back. She walked

up to me and picked at fluff and debris from the towels, as if protectively. "Do you want to go through the initiation ceremony? I'll understand if you don't, and escort you to the harbor myself."

Big honor. Did she know what I saw last night? Gabriel seemed to regret telling her that I'd trespassed. Maybe I'd left some clue behind. The bottle I saw him turning: he must've seen my fingerprints in the dust, and who else would dare enter? Therefore he'd had to tell her, out of fear that someone else might have noticed me first—without necessarily mentioning that I'd seen their ritual also, or knowing that I had. But maybe he told her everything, and if I said I didn't want to join, it was over for me.

"Look," Summer said. "Melodie's in the boat, primed to go."

Sure enough, she was—but that was meaningless.

I was far too weary now to summon the energy to lie further, to do anything other than what I truly wanted.

Because to stay now, knowing all that I did, seeing whatever inhabited my sister now, in the day and at night—what would I be doing it for?

It would be like hanging out with Grandpa in the late stage of his Alzheimer's. Whoever I loved had long departed and spending time with his body was just a tribute to the person who had once lived there.

"I want to stay."

To visit my sister's body like a tomb. Because it's all I had left.

The crowd cheered.

I looked at Joanna. No reaction.

"Okay then," Summer said. "Go to the throne and I'll get Patricia."

She was real?

I sat in the throne. The tentacles folded over me, squeezing my stomach.

Summer came back into view, the arm of a sedated old woman slung over her shoulder.

Patricia wore a diaphanous silk shift, her unwashed grey hair hanging on either side of her head. Deep lines covered her face. She moaned, revealing a scarcity of teeth.

Summer wouldn't let go of Patricia's arm as they walked together towards the stone. She unlocked the cover and pushed it back.

The crowd sighed with awe.

Summer held Patricia's wrists and had her reach out.

Scars ravaged the woman's palms. She grabbed onto the stone, which Summer supported by applying grip strength through Patricia's forearms.

The island's light died once again, the plants flopping into hibernation, their background hum diminished. Even the throne's tentacles fell to the side again.

The woman turned and walked slowly towards me, careful not to drop the stone.

Patricia moaned a series of vowels at me.

"She says to take the stone," Summer said.

"With my bare hands?"

Summer nodded.

I leaned towards it, seeing my face reflected in it like the metal sphere in an Escher portrait. The image distorted, dents and warps passing across its surface, as did stripes, like some camouflaging cuttlefish.

My hands reached out. Cracks on the stone's surface glowed. In one corner, I saw someone running along the table towards us.

A wave of outrage passed through the crowd. I ducked as Joanna flew towards us, tackling the women and grabbing the stone with her hands. It sizzled and she screamed, doubling over, crouching on the floor. Rust-colored smoke puffed out of her bent-over shape, on either side.

She turned and looked at me. "Go!"

I was on autopilot now, bolting towards the harbor, dodging the Glowfolk who didn't want me to go. They streamed on either side of us.

I tripped. Someone gripped my ankle. I turned to see Ella, and tried to wriggle away from her. As thin as she was, she was filled with strength. I kicked at her fingers where she gripped my leg, but she wouldn't relent.

Gabriel appeared and stamped on my leg—but only so he could grab Ella and wrench her off me. The pair wrestled and I was free again.

Joanna was soon alongside me, holding the stone like a rugby ball under one arm as we bolted towards the boats. She threw the ball at Melodie, who yelped.

"Give me the key and get out!" Joanna shouted at her.

Melodie pulled the cord from her wrist, shaking.

Behind us, the roar of approaching Glowfolk got louder.

"Quickly!" Joanna shouted.

Melodie whimpered, tossed the key at Joanna and clambered out the boat.

Joanna started the motor. It sputtered and the boat began to move.

A man jumped off the pier at us, his hand grabbing at the rim.

I pulled the fingers off, one by one. The boat wobbled as he fell into the water.

We sped away. As I looked back at the island, I saw Melodie standing there with her arms out in protest. The crowd ran at the harbor, ignoring her. A rogue shoulder knocked her into the water as the others dove in, as they filled the remaining boats.

As we returned to the mist, the island dissolved away once again. Glowfolk gathered by the harbor still, their distant white robes like pale piano keys. Some dropped their robes and piled into the water, determined to swim all the way back to land if that was what it took to return their power source.

The remaining handful of boats took off after us, but we maintained our head start.

The stone rolled towards Joanna. She scooped it beneath her legs, behind the back of her plastic tunic, which kept it away from her skin.

Even from so far away, the grief-wracked screams of Summer echoed off the walls of her snuffed-out island and across the sea.

The boat wavered left and right. Joanna's hand slipped on the steering handle, lubricated by her own blood.

"It doesn't hurt too much," she said. "Not anymore."

―――――

The pier emerged before us, as did the rusting carnival rides, the dilapidated buildings. It was a relief just to see land again.

Police squad cars and ambulances parked above the pier. A figure stood on the bonnet of one near us. It was Henry, watching us with binoculars. As we got nearer, he dropped them and sped along the pier towards us. There was no one else along it; likely it had been cleared for police business.

We docked at a slip and got out.

Henry walked up to us with open arms. He hugged me and smoothed my hair. I felt the rubbery grip of his gloves.

"You must be Joanna," he said over my shoulder.

"That's me," Joanna said.

Henry let go of me again.

Joanna took off her tunic and wrapped it around the stone. She stood wearing a wet cotton dress, looking up at the sky. "It's going to get dark soon."

"That's okay," Henry said. "Come with me. We've prepared everything you need."

We walked together, the three of us, Henry with his arm around me, Joanna by my side clutching the ball.

A crew of people in hazmat suits and facemasks waited for us at the end of the pier.

"What's this for?" I said.

"It's okay, Lily," Joanna said.

Two men knelt by the stairs leading off the pier.

Joanna handed them the stone. "This is it."

The men ran off with it. Two more appeared in the same place.

Joanna slouched and walked toward them. They grabbed her by the arms and carted her up.

"No!" I screamed. "Where are you taking her?"

Henry shushed me and held me close. "You'll see her again in no time. I promise."

I tried to kick free, but he wouldn't let me. I fell to my knees, in tears.

He took my hand. "Come and see. It's for her own good."

We walked up the stairs together. Bystanders gathered behind a barrier and watched, taking photos.

The hazmat guys had strapped Joanna to a gurney, which they held up and pushed into an ambulance. Purple light diffused through it, lamps buzzing harshly. UV light again.

I held Henry's gloved hand and let him guide me to his squad car.

It's going to get dark soon.

CHAPTER 15

We joined the ambulance at the hospital.

A kindly nurse guided me to a private room, where there was a chemical shower and examination table behind a curtain. By a computer was a blocky-looking device encased in white metal. Above a set of cabinets were a sharps box, a bottle of hand sanitizer and a glove dispensary.

I went behind a curtain and removed my wet clothes, passing them back to the nurse, who would incinerate them.

I took a mandatory chemical shower and got dressed in lilac scrubs with a teddy bear print, then I came back through the curtain. For shoes I had a pair of thin slippers, like the disposable ones found at cheap hotels.

"What's this?" The nurse said, holding up the plastic bag she'd taken from my jacket pocket.

"It's a sample of the island's plant."

She dropped it on the floor and stood back. "I'll let someone know and they'll get it looked at."

She asked permission to take a sample of my blood, a cotton swab of my mouth and scrapings from beneath my fingernails. All the samples went into a hatch in the metal

"What is it you're looking for?" I asked.

"We're calling it GRSE for the moment. Glow-related spongiform encephalopathy."

"Where have I heard that before?"

"It's caused by prions. You know, like Creutzfeldt-Jakob?"

I shook my head.

"Mad cow disease?"

My stomach sank.

The screen in front of her beeped and turned green. "You don't have it."

———

She guided me out the room and down the hall, leading me toward a different wing of the hospital.

The tests had taken so long that it was dark outside. As we pushed through two sets of double doors, the lighting got brighter, harsher.

She sat me down on a bench. Through the glass in front of me, she told me, was Joanna's quarantine. "They found traces of plastic in her stomach. You know anything about it?"

Maybe it had to do with becoming an EO. But I didn't know for sure, so I shook my head.

More sheets of opaque plastic separated me from Joanna —but there was a triangular gap at the bottom.

"You don't want to see," the nurse said.

I couldn't help it. I peered in.

Smock-clad doctors intubated Joanna. Some sat on chairs on either side of her and jabbed her with needles to put ports in her veins. I shuddered at the way the plastic tubes snaked towards her. The room's bright lighting enhanced how unnatural it looked. Big blinding white lamps set up in each corner connected a black extension reel that sat on the floor.

I recoiled, looking up and down the hallway. There were

multiple booths just like this one, masked by opaque plastic. A ward of Glowfolk.

"Your boyfriend will be back soon," the nurse said. "And a counsellor will come by later."

"Why?"

"It's best if he tells you. One thing at a time, dear."

"Are there others from the island here?"

She nodded. "In all these rooms."

I looked up and down the corridor. "I didn't know there were any other escapees still alive."

"Well," she said, "we believe they came from the island— but they can't talk anymore. We found them roaming the town." She touched my arm. "You're safe here though."

"But, wait."

The nurse turned.

I was so lost I didn't even know what more to ask.

She looked around. "Okay, I'm not supposed to." She took a phone out of her pocket and handed it to me. "I'll come back for it later."

"Thank you."

I used it to search for news about the island.

Live aerial footage showed the island in the dark. Three of its towers were on fire, yellow flames waving from them, giving off plumes of black smoke. Articles speculated about an accident occurring out there, but there were no names released yet. What would become of Patricia, Summer, Gabriel, Melodie?

Corinne had a new video up on The Switch, in which she interviewed Dennis Howell. He looked greasier than ever in the thumbnail. I'd have to pay to watch the full thing. I'd create an account for myself on one of my own devices when I was back with them again. For now, I had a brief preview video.

Dennis was uneasy having his authority questioned. "Our self-actualization task force has told you people time and again that we have no connection to that damn island. Our programs are flourishing. Of course this doesn't negatively impact our work. Beyond supporting the group's environmental initiatives, we're not associated with them at all."

"Our investigators traced the distribution of octadrone to your facilities," Corinne said. "The supply came from the island. What are you going to do now that—"

Dennis got up, tore his microphone off and walked away.

We'd surely harmed the Glow. Whether they'd claimed ownership of it, the impenetrable mystique of their island was their strongest symbol. One of the biggest reasons, surely, that few ever challenged them. Now it was ablaze across every major new outlet. Not only that, but as its supply of the drug that kept them all zombified, their brainwashing capabilities would take a major hit as well.

Only time would tell how badly. Did a movement ever die off when its leaders were taken out? Pernicious ideas were harder to kill than the people who came up with them.

I sank into the leather couch, wondering if I'd get a chance to tell Corinne in person what had happened to Heath before she had to read about it in some police report—provided there was any evidence left—and what I'd say to her if given the opportunity.

The weight of all I'd done and all I had left to do pressed down upon me at once. My mind shut down to deal with it all, sending me quickly to sleep.

CHAPTER 16

I woke to Henry looking over me. He'd loosened his tie and untucked his shirt. I winced at him with bleary eyes and sat up, giving him some space on the couch.

He touched my bare feet, warming them with his hands. "It's good to see you again."

"You too. Hey, why didn't you come out to the island?"

"Turns out better men have tried. They know all us cops. I might've scared the island away."

"They can send it into open water in under three minutes."

"So the rumors are true. All I could do was wait on land." He smiled. "Not to overwhelm you—but I don't know where any of this leaves us. All I'll say is that I'm sorry and you're welcome to return to the house. If you want."

"That's kind of you to offer. But it really depends."

He stopped stroking my feet. "On what?"

"What you're about to tell me."

He sat back and turned to me. "Are you ready?"

I wasn't, but I needed to hear it anyway. I nodded.

"The stone did come from space," he said.

I sat up. "Right."

"But it's not a meteorite as such." He bit his lip. "It's more like a bomb, filled with prions."

I winced. "They cause the disease. The GRSE."

"Exactly. And as far as the lab can tell, they're synthetic. Created to harm humans."

I laughed incredulously and swept hair out of my face with cold, tired hands. "What do you mean?"

"When the stone contacts human skin, it infects people with the prions."

My heart rate went up. "I saw something last night. A group of them on the island. They—devoured one of the visitors."

We sat in silence.

"What about the plants?" I said finally.

"The sample you provided—for one, it's jam-packed with octadrone. And it also seems designed to optimize our atmosphere for—whatever sent the stone in the first place."

I jerked as I heard a screech coming from Joanna's room—it was the sound of a nurse pulling back the plastic curtain. The doctors and other staff were leaving.

We paused and looked at Joanna. She sat up and stretched her arms towards me as far as she could, the handcuffs round her wrists clanging on the rails. She had a look on her face like a scared child. Like she wanted me to lift her and take her away from all this.

The little sister I knew. The one who had managed to overpower the Glow's ideology. The one whose inability to watch me join the Glow—to embark upon the same mistake to which she'd dedicated years of her life—overpowered her indoctrination. Even if it was only for that one instant, when she stole the stone, it sure as hell counted.

"She's infected, then," I said.

He nodded.

She seemed fine now. Because of the lights.

I wept, but I could feel that my expression was still stoic.

"Maybe it was just a test before some big attack. And it works, all right. I don't think it's the last of those devices that we'll ever see."

"Think of how it could've gone. If Patricia hadn't made the island, the stone would've gone straight into the water."

"Patricia had visions that told her to make the island first. It was a testing ground. A sample population. Prior to a full-scale attack."

"Well, whether that's the case, without your intervention, we wouldn't have gotten the chance to study the prions before the disease spread. They tell me there might be a gene that allows these prions to form in the infected. If that's the case, we can cut it out and immunize people."

"Can we immunize Joanna?"

I knew the answer. A black sea of loss rose through my mind, saturating all my memories of her.

Flirting with a vendor on the beach to score us free ice cream sandwiches. Crying over the kites at Club Med. Digging her teeth into the Ripper's ankle. If that had even happened.

Henry made to say something. He stopped, regrouped and held my face in his hands gently, as if cupping a flower's petals. "You were so brave." He laughed. "Thank God I didn't manage to stop you going there in the first place."

"You think you could've?"

He took his hands off me. "You did your best for Joanna. More than any sister could expect. Now it's time to come home."

"Sure." I grit my teeth and tried to remain strong, to ride the weird peace that accompanies the biggest shocks. I could break soon. I could finally let it all out. But I had to hold on, to steel myself for one final task.

"I just have to say goodbye for now."

He nodded solemnly.

I side-eyed him and added, "Alone."

He sighed, kissed me on the forehead and paced down the hall.

I got up, as if in a trance, and opened the quarantine door.

An alarm horn blared, even as I slammed the door behind me and pushed a chair beneath it from the inside.

I heard Henry's heels skid on the linoleum, and he ran up to the glass.

Joanna had her arms out still. Her face was dried out, cuts on her cheeks, dark circles around her eyes, lank hair. Plastic cables streamed from her arms.

Bang bang bang. I turned to the door. Henry was back, his fists pummeling at the window, terror in his eyes.

I looked at him through the corridor's warning light, each red pulse of it showing his panic, panic, panic.

I turned away and embraced Joanna. Her weary arms fell around me, her head collapsing onto my chest.

I kissed the top of her head, and turned out the lights.

ABOUT LEO X. ROBERTSON

Leo X. Robertson grew up in Glasgow, Scotland, met his husband in Gijon, Spain, and eventually moved to Stavanger, Norway, where he works as a process engineer, writes fiction, and makes short films with the Stavanger Filmmakers Club. An author of unclassifiable fiction that tends towards the dark and speculative, he has short stories published by *Helios Quarterly*, *Flame Tree Publishing*, and *Pulp Literature*, as well as novellas published by *Unnerving* and *Nihilism Revised*. On his podcast, *Losing the Plot*, in association with *Aphotic Realm* magazine, he interviews other authors about anything and everything (hence the show's title.)

He appears to be at work on numerous novels, short stories, and short film scripts. Also, he loves his sister dearly and, if necessary, would easily take a boat out to a plastic island and feign interest in joining a cult for her.

To find out more, follow him on Twitter @Leoxwrite or check out his website at leoxrobertson.wordpress.com

CPSIA information can be obtained
at www.ICGtesting.com
Printed in the USA
BVHW042158101122
651734BV00004B/41